The Way Back

The Way Back

ENRICO PALANDRI

translated by Stuart Hood

Library of Congress Catalogue Card Number: 92-60142

British Library Cataloguing in Publication Data
Palandri, Enrico
　Way Back.—(Masks Series)
　I. Title II. Hood, Stuart III. Series
　853.914[F]

ISBN 1-85242-246-7

The right of Enrico Palandri to be identified as author of this work has been asserted by him in accordance with the Copyright, Designs and Patents Act 1988

First published in Italy in 1990 as *La via del ritorno*.
Copyright © 1990 by Gruppo Editoriale Fabbri, Bompiani, Sonzogno, Etas S.p.A., Milan

Translation copyright © 1993 by Stuart Hood

This edition first published 1993 by
Serpent's Tail, 4 Blackstock Mews, London N4

Set in 11½/14pt Bembo by Contour Typesetters, of Southall, London
Printed in Denmark on acid-free paper by
Nørhaven A/S of Viborg

to a distant friend

The one who stays is moved by nostalgia
The one who leaves is held by nostalgia

Giacomo Noventa

to leave, to return

I

So we all meet in Rome. The evening before leaving again I went to eat at Turiddu's, there was Aldo Mansi, Walter Righi, Fernando, Sandra and Giacomo, at the end Fabio Cavalieri came as well. When there are these large gatherings at table Turiddu comes on like the conductor of an orchestra, pencil in hand held high over the heads of the customers, ready to bring in each voice from the general hubbub one by one with a nod of his head and collect the orders.

'So what shall I bring for starters? rigatoni alla paiata, fettuccine with tomatoes and basil, bucatini all' amatriciana?'

He slows down, repeats, underlines. He seems to be singing, savouring in advance the pleasure of his audience, whetting its appetite with intriguing details ('the endive is that good stuff from my cousin in Ceri'), inserting calculated, delicate *ritardandos* or imperceptible *rubatos* in his sustained solo until he has everyone in his grasp and can impart his advice magnanimously, certain that only a madman or an idiot could ask him for something other than what he is offering. In fact if someone who doesn't know him has the courage not to be seduced by any of his proposals and begins to turn over those pages of the menu which in a restaurant of this kind have a purely decorative function, Turiddu the host becomes Turiddu the Terrible: from under his thick black moustache he fires a fierce burst—'it's off,' 'no, we don't have it today,' 'you mean it's written there? well, maybe it's written down but there isn't any, that was the other day . . .'—until he erects an impenetrable wall of denials behind which he shields the honour of mothers and wives who from time immemorial have been watching over the rumbling cooking-pots and the precise way spaghetti turns *al dente*, the perfect consistency of a sauce, and if you don't like it you can always put your jacket on again and go back home.

Having dissuaded the rash customers who had ordered risotto and escalopes alla Milanese, Turiddu begins to write out the orders with the solemnity with which he might accept our last wills and testaments then disappears. Sometimes he pops up again at the end of the meal, with eyes that are veiled by a good-humoured melancholy and say it is time to shut up shop, the evening is over, let's go home, we are all tired, I hope you have eaten well and that you will come again, I hope so and can only hope so because I know very well that endive even it comes from Ceri is just endive! It is a restaurant that never becomes fashionable perhaps because of the extravagantly extrovert manners of the owner who is on first name terms with everyone.

We began with the usual pleasantries that people exchange when they haven't seen one another for some time, as they take their seats at the table: 'How are things?' 'Are you still in that job?' 'And Paolo? Still in America?' 'Did you hear that Alfredo wants to get the Mole going again?' Gradually the conversations pick up the threads of old and new understandings. Someone is looking across to where he didn't manage to get a seat, another is trying to make a conquest, another is describing the speciality of the house, another is fretting and thinking he'd have done better to accept another invitation and someone else is going back over when we last saw each other, where we were and what we ate, as if getting together again were the umpteenth instalment of a play we are all in and that those 'do you remember?'s called us back from the various roads we are taking in real life. Once this was Nicola's role but this evening he's not here.

Can I be the only one not to know what this Mole is that Alfredo wants to set up again: is it a newspaper? a restaurant? or is *to get the Mole going* some slang that I have forgotten? and this Alfredo, who is he? Fortunately, Aldo Mansi shrugs sceptically and I feel that I too am relieved of the duty of pursuing the matter further.

At the end of the table Giacomo is breaking the bread the way his father always used to do. With his eyes he was following the movements of all of us, without speaking, with that sureness and timidity with which cats move about in flats, disdainful, docile when caressed, but ready to spring into a defensive posture if they get the hint of a threat. He was sitting next to Sandra and something was not right about their gestures: he is a man by now, she still dresses and speaks like a girl. They had negotiated a truce, a tense, wearing, secret one: this evening the mother wants to be a woman; the son, simply Giacomo. So they had left home as two contemporaries, had sat down together, but continued to ask to be left in peace using their elbows, their glances, their 'please pass the water'. I was sitting opposite them and could not help noticing their unease. I had in mind the scar Sandra has at the back of her neck, I sought her scents. I noticed that I kept on avoiding her eyes and so had lost track of what was being said. I had lost myself in thinking about that scar, then about that long train journey I had just finished (I would take the plane to get back to London this time), about Julia, about the faces and what we talked about then: they called me back towards a place I had left at a certain moment. I watched the mouths around the table chewing bread and words, I felt as if we had all once been in some group photograph and that now, each of us, swallowed up in different worlds, each with their separate way of looking at the past, was climbing laboriously back towards that moment, swimming against the current, forcing ourselves to appear present with bursts of laughter, witty remarks, nods of the head. One only had to stop swimming for a second, as I had done, and the conversation passed one by, one found one's self in another time, as had continually happened to me in the train during this journey and was doing so again now at table with old friends.

Then Walter Righi laughs loudly, they are teasing Fernando about a reversible jacket—an unexpected touch to his dress. Fernando got up to show himself off and gave an embarrassed little bow to the table in an attempt to put an end to all the attention. I noticed that he was still wearing sandals and pointed them out to Aldo who smiled to me and nodded. Signs of the times, as they say, which leave traces on us and traces of traces and traces of traces of traces . . . Giacomo was too young to pick it up but for me and the others these sandals (so like the sandals of a friar) recalled a certain Franciscan attitude which a few years ago had always been the true vocation of people on the Left like Fernando. Those sandals filled my gap—I thought that in spite of the bitternesses, the tragedies and the disillusionments which had detached Fernando, like all of us, from these years, the chances which had thrown us in such different directions, these sandals remained connected to that period, indicated the point where a world had sunk out of sight leaving behind it this flotsam of forgotten things, new fashions, which in their turn bring people together before being sucked down to the bottom, into that silence where one no longer understands what certain words and ways of being meant. With that reference to Fernando's sandals I was saying to Aldo: That's where the past got out from, you can still see the hole.

Every so often someone asked me, 'Are you back in Rome? and what are you doing in London?' I replied vaguely, responded in my turn with similar questions and took part discreetly in the convivial superficiality of the conversation. We talked about the cinema, books, and finally about the amnesty. And naturally about Nicola. Some people have ended up believing that Nicola really killed someone and his wife Sandra is certainly among them but that was not what we talked about. Innocence becomes a private matter as with the years we gradually get used to all feeling a little guilty of something or other. From laziness, resignation, prudence one ends up bothering about others only when it is necessary to defend oneself and there is nothing so frightening as the hypothesis of their innocence because it would lay bare our misanthropy. Instead we talked about the outcome of the trial because now Nicola is a court sentence for those who knew him as well as for those who read about it in the papers. Years ago, around tables like this, people asked: But is he innocent or guilty? 'Nicola Santi? that's ridiculous,' said someone, we talked about repression, we signed petitions, others with a shake of the head told of episodes of fraternal solidarity with the victim. With the passage of weeks, of months and years the sentence had however acquired a certain substance—the evidence was inconsistent but thanks to the slowness of the proceedings was long-lasting or else was replaced by other pieces of evidence and it was difficult to keep up to date. The law took its course and a dust of distraction settled on the files of the trial, on the conversation of those who were indifferent and in the end even on that of his friends. Thus one evening, in order to turn the page, someone ventured to say: 'Fabio Cavalieri, certainly not, but I wouldn't put my hand in the fire for Nicola . . .' And who would put it there? Then for months no one saw him, how can one remember exactly what he thought and what he did when he was with us? So what people say, the slow-burning forge of public opinion, begins to imitate the strong and anonymous voice of the law. We begin by not putting our hand in the fire for anyone, and then later maybe that judge was right . . . Meantime if Nicola Santi's lawyer phones please tell him I'm not in.

At a certain point Fabio Cavalieri arrived too. Warmly welcomed he remained standing by the table and every so often went over and embraced someone, shook someone's hand, offered a cigarette. I didn't understand what people were talking about or perhaps pretended not to understand; he was Nicola's best friend and for a while, with that dismal fatalism—that hunch that, one after the other, friends and relations are being struck by misfortune—we all more or less expected to see his name in the papers. Instead he kept out of them. He went and sat next to Giacomo, clapped him on the shoulder and cast a furtive glance at Sandra. She, who had followed all his movements round the table, turned abruptly towards me and asked me, 'What do you mean?' as if she were resuming a conversation.

Giacomo did not even give Fabio the time to open his napkin: 'So you think my father is a murderer?'

'No, he isn't. He never picked up a weapon nor did he tell anyone to do so.'

Sandra suddenly abandoned our non-existent conversation, pushed Giacomo aside with her arm and interrupted Fabio with ferocious sarcasm, which came from away back: 'Poor thing, so dear Nicola talked about football with the Red Brigades and didn't notice they were shooting.'

'What has that got to do with it! He was a revolutionary and a leader.'

'And at any moment he could have taken us all to prison with him.'

'You didn't end up in prison and won't any more,' Fabio responded drily.

The other conversations had been interrupted. No one felt like telling Fabio that what they felt was that Nicola really was a murderer—or perhaps didn't feel like telling Sandra that her rancour towards Fabio Cavalieri had little to do with what Nicola might have done. Fabio asked for a light, then someone muttered something at the other end of the table, Sandra pretended once more that she had to tell me something and little by little, like the dry bundles of brushwood which catch fire in the hearth, crackling alone at first, slowly, and then rapidly and in chorus, the conversations spread out in the warmth of a single chorus of voices from which every so often there rose like a flame a yellow tongue of laughter or a piercing interjection. Supper over, on the way back to the cars, Fabio was arm-in-arm with Giacomo a few yards in front of me. He was telling him to come to Ancona, they would talk about Nicola.

'Nicola is not innocent—no one is—but don't be ashamed of him—try to understand him.' Fabio had lived with Sandra after Nicola left, he had been one of Giacomo's fathers.

Sandra was behind me and tried to get in front; she touched the arm Walter Righi held round her neck, like a prisoner adjusting her chain, and thrust her head forward in an attempt to catch some of what Giacomo and Fabio were saying to each other. Poor Sandra! Fabio noticed and quickened his step. I too, one summer some time ago, was Sandra's lover and recognised her particular way of walking along the street, excited by the furtive, unexpected glances of strangers, and blind to the feelings of the person close to her. As long as the person who is with her doesn't get tired of waiting for her this side of her blissful way of imagining that the world is benevolent, she feels protected and searches for something—but even she does not know what—behind the appearances, in the words, in what *they mean*. She looks at you with eyes that are pained and enchanted, incapable of believing that her feelings do not produce a universal echo and her disappointment at least makes one feel sorry and one ends up by asking her 'What can I do for you?' then one day one gets tired, as I got tired, as Fabio got tired, as this Walter will get tired sooner or later. One gets tired of speaking to the wind, to the fantastic tangle of her thoughts which are always fleeing from the here and now, of her being condemned to love only what is not there, the memory or the future, and one finds it better to speak to a cat.

Sandra wakes up and suddenly notices that she is alone, has always been alone. Her love was only a dream, was never anything other than a picture through which the other person walked, peopling her inmost places with events which now echo in her solitude. She would like to go through the world to give the sad, sad news: *no one loves me! no one has ever loved me!* But the world knows that; it is bored and shuns her, even vases fall from her hands and look at her in pieces from the floor. And she is so lost, she misses others like air, more than her own body of which she is hardly aware.

I hear your nervous steps behind me, your disjointed phrases. I have in mind the scar at the nape of your neck and would like to kiss it, Sandra of the impossible loves. I should like to stop and turn round, let you catch up with me and cross the years of distance and feigned indifference in which we met just by chance and hug you even if I know you would not understand. I should like to tell you that even if you can only love the one you do not have and so cannot love, I who saw you vanish into your melancholy and could not reach you loved you. But could you hear me? You are there torn between a love you have and do not want, another which you imagine you want again and all those possible encounters which disappear round corners. My voice would be confused with the echoes of your delusion along with all the possibilities which are now fading into each other in the dwindling future. Fabio too, in the three hundred yards that took us to the cars, must have remembered the continual alarms of your fragility. He knew that your ears sought his voice as one seeks breath on coming out of the water, as one wishes for life when one feels it is not there, and was making an effort not to lose the thread of what he was saying to Giacomo. So he let Walter continue to torture you with his 'Are you listening to me?'s. 'But of course I am listening to you. What were you saying? But please let's keep on walking and not be too far behind the others...' How you test your lovers! I think what Fabio's life must have been with you, for him who gives and gives, who puts everything into your life and sees it disappear, every day one has to begin again, yesterday has disappeared in a black hole. 'Do you love me now? say it again, say it again every day like a prayer!' And Fabio repeats he adores you, don't be afraid, and sees that nothing sates your thirst for certainty, which asks him for the impossible, to protect you from old age and from death and that it is precisely because you know this is not possible that you continue to ask him 'But how much? and for how long?' You would like to understand, to have faith, to try to explain yourself and to understand him, but now everything is dying around you in such haste, it disappears into the past, even your intentions become mixed up with the dreams and the lies. You ask for forgiveness, you beg them to let you try once again, one last time before your time comes to an end. You look at yourself in the mirror and it seems to you that there is no more time—or at least not as much as you thought and you don't want this. You still dress and speak like a girl but you are changed: there was something in your youth that is no longer there today, something that was deceptive. It was a challenge in your way of dressing and behaving, in the fullness of your body, in your sincere laughter, almost as if your blasphemy—because it is blasphemy not to love the person who is around—became incarnate when you were twenty in an absurd, paradoxical presence. You were always there and all whole, nice, open, and yet you were never there. It seemed so impossible that you should get old that even today—now only out of habit—when your women friends see you again they sooner or later repeat the same phrase, the only one which they know will really please you: 'Sandra, goodness, you never get any older.' It is not true, you know it from the glances of men and from how Giacomo's friends look at you but for a second you are consoled, you allow yourself to be warmed by the hope that for you, contrary to what you know and contrary to your own senses, youth is about to reappear, that life can appear before you once again with its hopes and mysteries. You think that in this next life you will be as happy as you have been and not so unhappy either and who knows what will happen if once again . . . there, one by one the echoes of what has happened in the past come back to ensnare you and you can't turn back, there is not another life like the one you would like and every day gives you a push forwards towards a future you no longer want. Every caress has carved out a regret, you miss everyone and everything. You touch your face, the skin slacker, the wrinkles where time will dig in and does not go away. Every day with your armour of cosmetics you inspect in the mirror the angles of your face caught between the art of your make-up and the terror of being sucked into one of these furrows.

You have caught up with Fabio—who knows what on earth he had to say to Giacomo, maybe whether he would like to see him more often, even if he would like to have him back home again. You wonder impatiently why we are all standing there, you talk wildly, you watch him looking for the car keys in his pocket, you think he has something to give you and hold out your open hand to take it. You follow him as he avoids your glance like a minefield, all your thoughts ask him *why*? and a few words escape you, a whisper: 'Come back whenever you like.' With unconscious prudence you managed to say it under your breath, distractedly, as if you were asking the time; you think that at most he will have picked up a tone of voice. But Fabio knows you, how can you deceive yourself that he does not feel your fever? He shakes it off as if you had poured shit over him. He knows very well that there is no end to your anguish. His eyes repeat to you the reproaches he made to you a thousand times and you, like a little girl, stick that luckless hand back in your pocket, biting your lips. You hear the echo of your quarrels come back, Fabio about to leave the house and with a voice that allows of no appeal, lecturing you: 'We have given already, signora, thanks all the same! we have tried already to shake you out of your monotony, we have already acted out partings and farewells, we've already had the tears, the hysteria, shall we try to behave like adults just once?' What can you say? You have been trying for a lifetime and it never works! You would like to disappear before he really does say something so cruel, you murmur an 'I'm sorry' you no longer even know for what or for whom. But you have polluted the air around us as well, Fabio comes out with 'Forget it' while we draw back embarrassed. But you did not even hear him, you were torturing yourself because you felt you had not said enough. Come back whenever you like, even supposing he heard it, even the concierge could say to him. You can allow yourself something more sincere, you can send a more precise signal, I am always waiting for you, it is not a life without you, my love, stay for tonight at least. Now you will say something, you search for calm within yourself. You look at him. You call him: 'Fabio.' Fabio looks at you, perhaps it isn't true that he was avoiding your glance, but he is so cold and distant. 'Fabio,' you repeat slowly, the syllables break up in your mouth and you are so naked in our midst, with your poor sorrows. And now he too reads you entirely, he finds in his arms once more your fear, your hair, he recalls them like a shirt turning up in a wardrobe, Fernando's sandals, these corners where we have said goodbye, a life we have already lived and do not cease living and which goes on continuing even when we no longer want it. His eyes become tender, perhaps he will kiss you. *Fabio, my love*, your heart whispers while he caresses the nape of your neck, he finds once again with his fingers the point where a sheet of metal almost beheaded you in a car accident, the scar which I too sought in my thoughts. You know he is saying goodbye but you are confused, you lose yourself in other embraces like this one after which he didn't go away, you think maybe he too is thinking that he loves you, that he is about to tell you so, as I say it to you now in my thoughts while I watch you credulously give way to your misunderstandings. And for a second, in your confused emotional state, you too find something again: the open-eyed dream you had at twenty—*there will be someone who will love me and make me happy!* The dream of a love. You think that to love, to die, to part, to come back, to leave and find each other again are more or less the same thing, so many proverbs say so! They are so many ways of feeling others . . . another will do, this evening, you will do for me. To feel that beyond the frost in which we feel the days run away around us, the vases that fall to the ground, those others who watch us, our body which is no longer like us, there is another person to whom all this can be given and said, who comes from another solitude and tells stories of that world. Another whom we shall miss and who will miss us, another with whom to confuse me and you, with whom to share time, thoughts, words, bread. And another who seemed to have gone off with all these pieces of us and who is there instead in every embrace, in our moments of abandon, another who is all the sense one can seek in things. Perhaps you whisper something in his ear as if you were kissing him, he replies under his breath, but you do not understand. He leaves you, gets into his car and in a second is already gone.

You look round you and in the silence you see that things continue to move out there. The car manoeuvres and drives off. Giacomo follows it with a couple of useless steps, keeping a hand on the door as if to accompany it. Walter is staring at you, he says something, he tells you again speaking of things you don't hear, how lonely you will be with him in an instant, then you hear him say to Giacomo:

'So what is this amnesty? either a person is guilty or a person is innocent, and if he is guilty let him pay.'

'I think my father has paid enough already,' said Giacomo and Sandra took his hand and hugged him, and wept for all of us, children without father or mother abandoned on this earth.

II

The train had stopped at Varzo, near Domodossola. It was a summer afternoon. We had left Victoria Station the day before, that night I had slept little and badly. Some old men were playing cards under a pergola in the courtyard of a bar behind the station. They were arguing, sometimes animatedly. I did not catch what they were saying, I pricked my ears but they were a long way off beyond wire-netting brown with rust. I wrote in a notebook: 'Dear Italy, where people talk!'

I lost the notebook later but I remember this sentence because one evening, a year later, Julia read it out to me at Edinbane on the Isle of Skye; we had been wandering about for some days in the Highlands and in all the pubs we had found men, alone and silent over a pint of beer. The television set, always switched on on a bracket in a corner of the room, carried news from a remote world with different lights, different climates, and the exaggerated joviality of the presenters, the quiz competitors, sellers of soap-powders, journalists, politicians, a joviality which, seen from up there had something unreal about it. These truncated figures, talking at the tops of their voices, gaudy, looked like prisoners of something more mute than silence. One can get beyond silence, one can begin to talk or to make a gesture which reaches someone: the gabbling—the jolly and slightly hysterical gabbling of these people cut itself off however, wrapping itself up in a solitary logorrhea, it seemed like the remains of a world adrift trying to find the inlet in which to disembark its army of salesmen. The men in the pub drank their beer alone but no one watched the television which was thus merely an amulet, a little magic shrine to modernity put there to protect their silence, to affirm the gratuitous nature of any discourse.

Not that the Scots don't like to have parties—on the contrary, they have them only on ritual occasions: at weddings, which in Caithness last three days (on the other hand if someone makes the journey up there you certainly can't send them back after the ceremony) or at the splendid country Hogmanays with the first footing —that is the first visit to the neighbours and with people being found drunk in the fields as much as a week later, sometimes still singing, at other times frozen to death. And above all on the long winter nights round the fire with a glass of whisky in one's hand telling about journeys made, reciting poetry.

We talked about it a bit—I told Julia about the old men at Varzo, she told me about her childhood in Scotland, how she had felt repressed and frustrated among the puritans and how Italy had always seemed a happy country to her. While I listened to her describing the splendid qualities of my country I said to myself that she was biased, other utopias were awakening in her enthusiasm. But Julia was not to be stopped, without realising it I had already been caught up in her flow and was following her: Todi, Venice, even certain bars on the outskirts of Bologna took on mythical importance in her words. She had only once been to Italy, on her honeymoon, but since then she had not missed a film with anything to do with Italy and had read almost all the little of our literature she could find in translation. She knew by heart many opera arias and knew what they meant but the sense of the things and the words with which we say them had never really come together for her. This was another reason why for some months she had begun to study Italian and now spoke a smattering, slowly. But my country had remained a fantasy for her; the things she began to say, starting with the phrase in my notebook, was one of the first efforts she made to go beyond cautious comprehension and the correct pronunciation of the words; she had finally entered a different region, the one round which she had spun so many fantasies and which she had in this way sought out, constructed. She seemed one of those who arrive for the first time in company of which they have a high opinion and, fearing to appear inadequate, weigh each word and each gesture until, finding something familiar, they feel at their ease, recognise their world in that other world. That phrase seemed to her something that only an Italian could say about Italy and she was happy to understand it. She was at last on familiar terms with the oddities of my behaviour which, rightly or wrongly, she had classified as Italian, she felt superior to her old prejudices, no longer attracted by a mysterious exoticism but in a new house, in short she began to move around in her feeling of being Italian, to live in it.

I kept at bay nostalgia for the delightful country of Julia's words, muttering, making things clear, applying the brakes. But there was also a feeling of tenderness with which I replied to her, a strange homesickness, and that was what the phrase Julia had taken from my notebook and had woven into her enthusiasm came from. I looked at her with surprise and suspicion; I felt I had written something banal in an excess of sentimentality, but what right had I to rob those words of the meanings she had found there, in order to impose my scepticism? What right had I to say: Don't be silly. Look—Italy isn't like that, that phrase is mere stupidity, it is you who are making a romance out of it. Does what we say not always go beyond ourselves and our opinions? In the words we exchange, in the way we behave when with others, in a no-man's land where our frontiers intersect? What do we know about what we know, if not that along the way we find it, lose it and find it again continually?

Julia kept her eyes half-shut as if she were making an effort to see her Italy in the distance, to make it closer through her imagination, and in this she was so far ahead of me! Then she began to look at me again, seeking in my look confirmation of her fantasy, but I too by now was carried away by the enthusiasm with which she imagined my country. In her enthusiasm she projected on to me a *you, my Italian love, who did not have a hard puritanical childhood but grew up between hills covered with vines and the blue sea!*, and the tar which took the skin off my knees in my courtyards, the smell of cats and soup in the damp staircases of my childhood allowed themselves to get a high from her colours.

I adjusted the cushion behind my back, it was my turn to say something: 'Italy . . .' I began, continuing in the tone of her story. I had always been on my guard against nostalgia for my country as if against a fit of mourning and remained silent for a short while, searching for words, suspended between something I had somehow lost interest in and the beautiful descriptions Julia had given of the Italy I wished to make my own.

On this island we felt far from everything. Our brief holiday had already deleted the London timetables, the hospital and the theatres, we had immersed ourselves in a time that was ours alone, in which we did not need to answer the telephone, anyone, where we flew along together like two birds. Every so often the wind threw a handful of raindrops against the window and we stopped to make out the noises of the rain: a car coming nearer, a door banging, the distant barking of a dog. Julia, who when talking had held her bust erect, sustained by the excitement of her story, relaxed the muscles of her back, waiting for me to begin to speak. Who knows how much of what I fell in love with in her was only the taste of the foreign country through which she drove me; ideas about nature, society and the universe brought to the British isles by nomadic and warrior peoples: the Saxons, the Danes, the Celts, the Vikings, the Normans, the Picts. And naturally the Romans. Certainly the Picts bore the same relation to her as the blue sea to my courtyards, but at this point it was clear that with my clarifications I didn't so much hold her flow at bay as my own emotion. I gave way, thought by thought, from admiration to affection, from the intellect to love, in short I drew close to what there really was between us. An unusual transparency had been created, we talked and we looked at each other as if for the first time—but without the fear one usually has of unknown people. Shortly we would return to a familiarity that had no contours, enmeshed in the exasperating shortcomings of daily life, we would begin once more to swap crazes and whims, annoyances and courtesies, but now I saw it, saw the vein of gold which I had guessed at in her one day on one of Potter's buses and which had made me fall in love, and even the flaw which one day might lose her for me. I knew very clearly why I was there with her on an island where I had neither past nor future, and it was from there that I should have liked to put things to rights. Courage then, don't let us rob her of a future she doesn't ask for and which perhaps will never exist. 'Italy...' I repeated but did not continue. We smiled together at this, my second embarrassed beginning, but in that silence I saw so much road run past and was convinced she understood. I no longer wanted to say to her: Don't be silly. On the contrary, in the way we smiled together I felt our wings, perhaps we would never be able to see them but we were flying. No more clarifications, nor suspicions, but the dense atmosphere of your friendship. But I did not even manage to say this to you: I was afraid of drowning my hopes, of which there were so many, in excessive explicitness and so I was silent.

Once more I sought to establish a distance, confessed that my passions were banal, pasta, red wine, there are lots like me in Italy! Then I began to tell her once more about Varzo, playing the Italian, accepting to be typecast by those traits which among fellow-Italians are mocked good humouredly. I said that this habit of talking which the Italians have is the root of provincialism which, for good or bad, characterises us. That we often speak not to say something but to indicate a presence. And that was how I talked too, or rather how certain things talked by themselves. Something happened to me similar to what I had noticed in Julia when she had stumbled into her first real statement in Italian: a world that was secretly frequented began to speak: I pricked up my ears as I did that afternoon in Varzo to listen to the old men, but I was immediately lost, or perhaps rediscovered, in an unfathomable number of resemblances, differences, memories. The words called to each other and in this way spoke themselves; I did not even manage to put names to them all, to understand how they were connected to each other; I followed them, caught up in their current. Then I went back to Varzo, to the afternoon of last summer.

Even if I had been able to hear those old men I wouldn't have understood much, the dialects of Lombardy, you see, are incomprehensible to me. And even if I had understood, if I had got off the train, had gone up to them and had begun to speak, from my accent, from the very fact of my addressing them as if of right, they would have understood that I was not from these parts, and would have answered me in another language, in the Italian of school, of military service, of TV and the office. This too I had known at a certain point in my life: in Rome, as a boy, with my schoolmates, sons of people from the Veneto, Sicily, Turin, Naples, catapulted like me into that strange Italian in which the dialects of our parents and grandparents were dying. Anyone who had a native language knew that this was a foreign language and anyone like me who did not have one could not distinguish the Italian words from the remnants of dialect which wandered through our sentences; so we all spoke by trial and error, a language of fragments. The grammar we learnt in school was only a hypothesis, another, umpteenth language which was used in books and for elegant conversation. And yet there were no classrooms, we went to school in shifts and in packed classes, with teachers lost in their turn between the Fascist education they had received and the antifascist Italy which they had to teach us to love and respect, men and women whose childhood had been swallowed up by the war and who, looking at us, often did not know what to teach. Our real school was rather that society unexpectedly uprooted from its provincial, peasant and patriarchal origins, and projected into the general enthusiasm of the boom.

Now I too was aware of an Italian tone—that irony about one's own misfortunes which makes us resemble each other, to say what we are thinking. Julia and I usually did not talk like this; the Italian voice which had wakened in me turned, rushed back in haste, unconscious and enthusiastic; to find arguments and contexts restored to it a certain density and at the end of that rush I imagined a joy, or at least the end of a pain. I'd have liked to tell Julia about the park, about Livio, Nerina, about everything and everyone. Instead I had stopped again with a lump in my throat. The Italian voice simply had not reached out to her to tell a story, it had got stuck in a hole behind the vocal chords with suffocated cries. I thought that fifty years ago with the same superficial patriotic enthusiasm my country would have sent me to kill Julia, the men in that pub, while those whom I imagined to be my allies were exterminating my family in Treblinka. I spoke no more, I saw running through my head trains laden with people, the grandparents I had never known, the uncles and aunts, all those people of whom only the names remained for me. I thought of my mother who at sixteen escapes from Warsaw, not even knowing whether to the east or the south. I thought of my religious lessons in the corridor, my mates who shouted: 'Hey, Polack, pass that ball!' How much I should have liked really to be a Pole sometimes. But then why speak of Italy? Did that blood not suffice for me? I saw the words I had just said disperse in watery rivulets, get lost in an enclosed void within me where all I wanted was revenge. But on whom? And why? My mother had long since completely hidden all traces of her origins from our life, to be Italian had always seemed to me rather obvious and accidental. Now I was confused by my strange nostalgia; the more anger brought to my lips a lament for Italy, the more intimately I was aware how painful that distance, the time and the miles between me and my country, had suddenly become. What am I doing up here in the Hebrides, so far from home?

Julia was looking at me with a puzzled expression, perhaps a little bored. I felt condemned: everything I had lived through, the errors and attempts that had brought me up here, to be what I was, had become invisible, wrapped with me in a shadow of silence. By talking I would no longer cross the path of what she or anyone else was saying, I would have stitched on to me the hysterical chatter of someone talking to himself, I would have become one of those television sets that are left turned on in pubs. With my eyes I measured an exasperating distance between Julia and me, I tried to cross it with a few sentences, but all the words disappeared in my thoughts, I was afraid of not being able to hide anything any more and of not being able to say far less explain it. We were flying together, now I had crashed to the ground, I had ended up by repeating for myself the walls of which I knew I have always been prisoner. That was something else I had known and had forgotten—not to think about Italy, not to talk about it. But what on earth could I explain to her? My life down there was lost amid memories so intense and confused that every word was deflected by them while I was thrust further back by each of these vain words into a silent world. If something I did had offended Julia now I would have lost her, the distance that had been created between us was our radical difference—something from which we would never be free, the language in which we had learned to know the world and from which so much of us still poured forth. Certainly it was a miracle that, coming from places so far apart, our lives had crossed at a certain point; and I who do not believe in miracles saw clearly that this meeting at that moment as at every other was fragile, played out on the cusp of incomprehension, of the inability to have any exchange, as if to each phrase spoken the other could retort: I do not understand, it all stays inside you, nothing comes out, you are mad—thus shutting him up in his world once more.

She pushed her fringe away from her eyes with another smile which said I do not understand and I was missing her. She had the humble look people take on in a foreign language when they have not understood a word and indicate this without wishing to force the speaker to repeat: let him judge whether it is worthwhile or whether we are even capable of following what he is trying to say. I was still trapped in the depths of my introverted obstinacy, which was angry and loving but shut off, incommunicable. Julia had perhaps not noticed, perhaps she had, in any case she was there asking me with her eyes: I didn't understand, do you want to try again?

Right, I am not a book or a television set, you can ask me and I answer you. I remained silent for a few more seconds holding back in my throat the shouts of protest and the words of excuse and sought for the thread of the conversation, Varzo, that story you were pursuing, Julia, and which held together our lack of understanding. Varzo... The air was still as often happens in Italy in summer, the world motionless. From a window near the station there issued music from one of those little radios that seem more conscious of the boxful of transistors than of the music. There was also the voice of a woman singing along with the radio, probably in the same room. I leant from the window, I even think I singled out the window from which music and voice came—the one with the shutters wide open and carpets on the window sill, but I did not see the woman. It was a strong voice, out of tune, young, probably annoying for everyone, but not for me, not for me at that moment because it spoke to me of home, of that lost fatherland which I have wept for from the first day of my life and which I then sought, constructed in my heart, in my language. It spoke to me of Rome, of cleaners in the blocks of flats in summers like this so many years ago and of Nerina.

Into the carriage came a customs officer who immediately calmed my feelings of nostalgia. For a moment I thought of embracing him but I didn't have time: with almost unconsciously mechanical gestures I had already opened my suitcase for him and now watched him rummage among my underpants. He spoke with the arrogant tone policemen adopt when they think there is something not quite right between you and the law. He must have been about twenty but I was unable to recognise the accent he had learned to disguise, at least in these rapid verbal exchanges, with anonymous, authoritarian, rapid expressions: 'Passport,' 'Nothing to declare?' he spoke Italian in bites, as if with each phrase he let a guillotine come down between the peasant he came from and the bureaucrat he was heading for. When he addressed me more directly he used exclusively imperatives: 'Don't worry,' 'Open this,' 'Leave it alone' without ever adding a please or thank you, not even one of these purely ritual ones to which I had become pleasantly accustomed in England. With a little regret I thought, he was the first Italian I was seeing, I wanted to hug him, but that was out of the question. I stared at him while he searched with his head thrust into my suitcase, I was suddenly at the mercy of his whims and could not but follow every gesture of his as if I already had the handcuffs on my wrists. In the windless air outside the train every motorcycle engine, every banging door, called me home and the woman who was singing had begun to beat her carpets and now I could have seen her while from the little table with the old men there had risen a chorus of curses and protests for a card badly played and now one could hear every word: 'Shit! Damn! Idiot! Prick! Is that how you play a trump?'

After having meticulously taken my luggage apart he asked me: 'What sort of job do you have?' He was clearly trying to find something not quite right about me. I got annoyed and replied: 'None.' I'm not sure if he would have believed I was a doctor. All I had was the face of someone who looked as if he hadn't slept all night and hadn't got rich. We looked each other in the eye for a moment: he did not believe me, obviously, and was wondering whether to make me leave the train; probably he was weighing up whether it was worth while investigating or if I were only out to make trouble. I was in his hands: he could, if he wanted, now make my return to Italy very unpleasant. I too was thinking things over: I regretted having answered him in that way, I had made myself stupidly vulnerable, as if I had wanted to challenge him. He had black hair and eyes, thick brows, a broken front tooth and large square hands with a big, scratched gold ring. He held my passport open in one hand and used it as a fan, striking it lightly on the palm of the other. I did not know whether he would detain me but I clearly saw another reason why I was sorry to have replied in that way: I had had my revenge, I had humiliated him. He could opt out of being a man facing a man by means of his uniform, by treating me as a criminal solely because I was crossing a frontier. I had had recourse to another kind of impersonality, that of class relations, by pretending to be someone who does not need to work to earn his living, thus magnifying the difference there was between us when we walked along the street in civilian clothes. I was sorry—I knew from his brusque embarrassed manners, from his undigested mouthfuls of Italian, what an effort he must make every morning to get into that uniform. Certainly he was not from Lombardy and who knows what story had brought him to this part of the country—in a way not so different from so many of his fellow countrymen—who had come north to Varzo to be a customs officer, perhaps on a salary lower than theirs. Had he come into hospital in London and told me that he had strange pains in the evening, he couldn't say where, I would have let him go on speaking about the cold, the food, the people who were too reserved, and would have made for him the diagnosis that he had written on his face: You are homesick. What they had taught at the customs officers' school barely masked the hostility he had felt for generations towards everyone who was not from his part of the country. He was another inadequately Italian Italian, as we had all been at school, confronted by that mysterious language so distant from our own real language, as we all were in terms of politics, faced by television and newspapers, always lost between that little social nucleus in which we had learned to know the world and a huge Italy where what we had learned was of little use. What a difference from the policemen of northern Europe with their orderly frontiers, their courteous and murderous precision. Like me that boy had left some years before in search of a job and, alone, in a country almost foreign to him, kicked against the pricks, filling with his own arrogance his distance from the others in order to feel like the protagonist in a situation where instead he was the victim. I had betrayed him, I had chased him back into his solitude, to his off-duty walks where his contemporaries, who do not wear a uniform even in the cut of their hair, avoided him when he was in civilian clothes as if he were an alien. I had once more presented to his eyes the graffiti on the walls that told him to go back to the South, the same things that in London told me and so many others that this was no place for us. I opened my arms, I'm not sure whether to clasp him to my heart or to beg his pardon on my behalf and on behalf of everyone that made up his life and this world, he shyly lowered his eyes, slammed my passport on my chest and scurried into the corridor and then down off the train.

I sat down, I looked once more at the old men who continued to play surrounded now by a knot of people who followed the game in silence. On the other side of the station a man of about forty in shorts and T-shirt came out of a little gate on his scooter with a big bottle in a shopping net slung on the handlebars. Then the train moved, I looked at the window from which the music was coming and saw a woman pull in a carpet; we went past other houses, high and low, and almost at once the countryside began. This country, which is painfully mine, I had left some years before with my head full of ideas, mostly confused ones. Did I know what was hidden away in my departure? Certainly if I ever did know I could not say it to myself, the baggage from those years was too heavy. I probably talked about curiosity and openings rather than about terrorism and unemployment. Not that, now that I was returning, I had clearer ideas about what I was doing, if anything I had got used to a certain state of not knowing. And then there was you, Julia, so I was coming back to Italy but I was leaving London.

Julia lay down at my side, took the watch from the bedside table, and showed it to me: it was three in the morning. She said something else, in English this time, which I don't remember exactly but the sense of which was something like this: the past is always in mourning, it is dead, finished. Youth, our roots, yesterday. But today we are talking and it is precisely that death which has set us free in the present, capable of loving, fighting, even of feeling regret without being sucked far away from things. This is Edinbane, today. And then she said in Italian: 'So you see we aren't strangers,' and her voice, still uncertain over the phonetics of my language, with double vowels, misplaced fricatives, a glottal stop which had exploded in her mouth as if in a Germanic language, crossed all frontiers. It was the language of all those many boys with whom I had been a boy who didn't know how to speak Italian and in my heart it was as the ancient lyric says: *Just here in my heart Eros gave shape to Eliodora who talks sweetly to me, soul of my soul*. She was my house, my country, she who each day was more at home in this other house of mine, my language, Italian. She had already shut her eyes and turned out the light, she was falling asleep quickly. I thought anew of that train which goes through the green Lombard countryside, among the ranks of poplars, amid the smell of cut grass, to find my friends again, some streets I haven't seen for so long and that bar at Sant' Eustachio where once upon a time they made good coffee. Who knows if that place is still there . . .

III

The train was crossing Picardy; some passengers had got on at Calais, I saw them wandering about in the corridor and looking into the compartments, suitcase in hand, searching for a place and I thought of Nicola. Some days before he fled from Rome the police had searched his house at dawn. I saw him, Sandra and Giacomo in the corridor in the house in via Capo d'Africa, covered by guns, and Superintendent Alfonsi who every so often calls Nicola into a room to ask him to explain *what these papers are*? They search in the drawers, unearth school jotters, notes on interminable and exceedingly boring meetings, photos of relatives and friends, fragments of times that had disappeared and had dug lairs for themselves in the drawers. Nicola, finding in his hands certain yellowed faces, thinks he had thrown them away earlier or lost them and that in any case he doesn't want them any more, that they can only contribute to making the past still more remote, that we must condemn it to sink into the mist where it becomes confused with what never was, with the ghosts of drunkards and the images of sleep. But had he not thought and done all this once before? It is as if time, rebelling, had escaped by finding a way of its own through the undergrowth of the inessential objects in the house only to turn up again unexpectedly before his eyes and the eyes of Superintendent Alfonsi. In the drawers, under the indifference, the neglect, where its meaning hides from a practised glance, there lives a discourse that replies to the questions of the judge. Sandra probably thought right away that Nicola was guilty: she cannot make out of what, but if the police are there he is guilty and she is too. There come to her mind ridiculous trangressions, going through a red light the week before, her lovers, past and future, as if the police were there to investigate her married life, and she makes confession silently to the barrel of the pistol they are pointing at her. They are not looking for her but she is ready to recognise herself in what they are seeking. Nicola feels more calm but is unable to explain himself. Every so often the superintendent casts glances at him and Nicola sees in them the chance to show his own calm, the serenity of someone who puts his trust in the solidity of the life he lives and knows how to rise above incidents like this without raging at the bureaucrats' chaotic poking about in his books and the things of his world whose language in any case they cannot grasp. But this calm he conceives of only in his imagination, he no sooner tries to speak than he hears how his voice breaks, offended, frightened, caught up in the violent gesticulations of this invasion. 'Put your hands above your head. Is there anyone in there?' One of them has found somewhere or other a notebook of poems by Agostino . . . how to explain them? They are sentimental poems, certainly, full of rhyming couplets, steeped in a naive Jacobinism where every so often the names of Gramsci and Marx appear in order to please me. I had not read either of them yet but probably I had already explained them to him. Agostino wrote songs for the guitar and he liked Marx because he rhymed with all the words that had a stress on the last syllable and ended in a. There isn't even a date here but we will have been thirteen or fourteen . . . The superintendent listens and doesn't listen, he adds the notebook to a pile of periodicals, newspapers, private letters. Nicola knows he cannot explain, it is too complicated and things cannot be looked at separately one by one, it is too abstract; one would have to go back to those times and perhaps even that would not suffice. He follows bit by bit the way they examine his house, they leaf through all the books, look in the umbrella stand, on top of the bookcases, behind the wardrobes, they examine each object as if they were stripping the flesh of the inhabitants' life from the furniture, from the pottery, from the masks bought in Venice in 1974 ('74 or '75?), Toti and Pilar's castanets, the love letters, everything we should have said and have never said and which inhabited this house like a ghost, a possibility still present in the future, the chance to settle accounts. Instead there pop out insignificant details which contrive to be overlooked during the investigation and end up by saying what the judges want. He touches his ear and is aware that he is betraying to them and to himself a nervous fear, all tense in anticipation of the conclusions the magistrates will form about his life. Then reading these notes, Agostino's poems, discussing the authors who make up my library and the evidence of someone or other, a presumed friend of mine, what conclusion will you come to? And will you be right? Or will you only have the strength? Or perhaps not even that and my case will be forgotten among so many others until the waters have calmed down? Shall I simply be another file in constant transit from one office to another as the bureaucracy ruminates? Meantime the years continue to come out of the drawers, scattered chaotically on the bed and then piled in a big box which the police will take to headquarters.

Each day passed, each doubt laid aside, is now exposed to the dark eyes of the pistols and submachineguns. And if they can plunder what he has forgotten, if he can no longer hide anywhere because everything is exposed, what is left to him? He must escape. He thinks this suddenly, without reflecting, like the inevitable consequence of what is happening in his house. When the wood burns the animals abandon their lair, run towards where the fire ends beyond the river, across the frontier. He looks at the bottles of herbs, the salt, the pepper on the kitchen shelves, the washing machine under the window, the television in the living room. How long have they been living like this?: with Giacomo crying, Sandra being unfaithful to him and everything always coming back to normal, reabsorbed by these walls, condemned to remain fixed like this until a divorce, tomorrow, in a month or ten years. In its anonymous and implacable order the flat had begun to crush them even before they brought in the furniture, ever since they had decided to buy it, to get married to please their families and sort themselves out. With the years it has reduced them to a silence of bills to be paid, jobs to do, unworthy and unending squalid little problems, endearments which corroded the tenderness with which once they spoke so as to make it impossible for them to say anything more. Even the chaos of this house-search could be dealt with, their little obsessions return to gleam frostily, unwished for, on the floor-tiles shining with wax, everything could find its place on the shelves and in the drawers and even they, like two washed-out rags, could start once more to poke at each other with little idiocies in the attempt to interrupt the indifference in which everything flows past within these walls. For a second he feels sorry for Sandra, who is holding her stomach with her arms, and for Giacomo, who is hanging on to his mother's skirt as usual. He feels that he, too, is absorbing and reproducing the violence done to them by this armed incursion, he would like to say to both of them, 'Keep calm, nothing will happen.' But his intentions fade away into the void, he finds her horrible, he knows that his wife is repeating by heart the usual complaints, he sees her shouting at him with her eyes *it's your fault* in order to save herself, as she does, convinced that if one thinks of oneself one can even survive the atomic bomb. He is aware of her rancour as if she were whispering it to him between her lips, avoiding a kiss, pushing him from the bed, leaving him to search for reasons while she sleeps. To embrace her in a moment will be to throw himself among the briars, and yet the police have left and now they are in bed, all three together, with Giacomo still holding on to his mother and Nicola caressing her and saying just this: 'Keep calm, nothing is going to happen.' His voice does not break any more as with the superintendent, it remains calm, firm, and he feels how Sandra trusts it and begins to cry. Even he no longer knows what he is saying, he reassures her, absentmindedly, hoping that the voice speaking from his throat can see further ahead than he can, maybe their future. Perhaps, once the violence is forgotten and the weapons pointed at them, the judges' doubts resolved, it could really be like this: he himself innocent, the bills paid, all of them happy and content. But today this voice is so unfamiliar that Nicola does not recognise it, it is the voice of what could have been their life if he had not fled. The disorder of things after the house-search, all that past violated, interrogated, taken to pieces to fit into some judicial theorem, their lives reduced to evidence against themselves, and they abandoned on this bed, robbed of the support of memory, forced from now on into an existence with no weight, no history, unable to look back because there is no longer anything to produce, nothing more to explain, everything has been scattered on the floor, exposed, selected and is now in the hands of the judges. The flat, that life, is now uninhabitable and Nicola is already following trains in his imagination, calculating journeys, studying itineraries. Sandra is weeping, she gets up, dries her eyes with her arm, picks up some things from the floor, puts a shirt sleeve back in a drawer and shuts it. How long will they be able to last? The shirts? The towels? The books on the shelves? The things in their places? How long until another gust of wind upsets them? But at least she has pity on them, rearranges them, as was foreseeable even when this house-search means that his days are counted, that he will have to justify choices made and not made, mysterious coincidences, mistakes, everything that makes up everybody's life but not when faced by someone who wants to understand: he will have to explain to someone who wants to entrap him. In a country where there are people who fire from hiding places, people want the law too to come out of its hiding place and reply like an avenger, to flush the assassins out of their lair, to make logical and peaceful what today is irrational and violent. But Sandra has pity for things, she gathers up the pants and vests just the same, puts them back in the drawers, puts the covers back on the furniture, puts the books straight in the bookcases, buries even these moments, the last of their life together. Nicola looks at her and sees that Sandra is merely frightened. He would like to warn her, in the name of an old understanding, tell her that in any case time survives on its own, to show her how the drawers spit out years of blood. He would like to explain and instead murmurs only; 'Leave it—come here.' She comes back close to him in the bed and whispers in tears, 'If only we had had more time.'

Yes, this is the end of their marriage. Sandra now thinks that the police did really come to announce it. She is ready to confess, even to him, that their life together has ended in a disaster and hopes, in silence, that at least the regret for their failure can be shared, that it is their farewell. Nicola will take a train as soon as possible and now thinks only of that. Perhaps he ought to be able to stay but his flight has already begun, by crossing the threshold the police have occupied every corner of his mind. Far from appearing calm, he had been expecting them for ages; the moment he saw them he felt his head shrink, his thoughts flatten against the walls of his consciousness, dwindle and disappear. He no longer thinks of anything, he is aware only of the stink of fear. With a sudden change of direction events have outlawed him, or perhaps he has discovered only now that he has always been an outlaw or perhaps the law doesn't come into it at all and he has simply realised that things are going to end badly. Or perhaps or perhaps or perhaps . . . what counts at this moment? It seems to him that there is nothing left to defend, nothing more to say, neither within him nor outside of him, neither for nor against. Somewhere else will certainly be no better than prison but in any case he is not making the choice. Circumstances give him so little space that perhaps it is they, the judges, who are putting him on the train so as to be able to seize him while he is escaping. *And why is he escaping if he is innocent?* For a good while he has not belonged to an organisation, he is alone faced by old things that turn up again, there is no one who can help him. There is not even anyone with whom he can talk about things. He has to restrain his anger and not allow his emotions to upset him; he still has his hands free and even his passport. But meantime some of the objects and clothes on the floor go straight into a little suitcase which is hurriedly filled, and Sandra weeps, weeps all the time, and he, stammering, mechanically repeats his 'don't cry' without even knowing any more if he is really talking to her. She says 'You're gone already', he no longer replies. And yet you only have to think about it—there is no choice, now that people have lost their heads, demand revenge, there is so much shooting, one doesn't even know who is shooting at whom. And the ambushes? And the bombs on the trains? And the massacres? what folly to try to explain. There is no one who can be accused of all this, and no society could seek justice at this moment. Faced by so much horror it is easy to become monsters, and if it is not possible to discover who is guilty of what, it is not difficult to punish: first they put you inside, then they explain.

Amiens. In an hour we will be in Paris. Who knows whether Nicola really ran away like this. Then we were all fleeing from those years, both murderers and victims, thrown together in panic and anxious over any sort of future. In the corridor of the train people go past suitcase in hand, some come from afar: Africa, Asia, Eastern Europe. Perhaps they too are fleeing from failed—or successful—revolutions, from war and from hunger in search of a quiet spot for a while.

the lost days

I

It is a crystal-clear night, without a moon, the other travellers are sleeping. The headlights of a car or the light from a window from time to time illuminate a fragment of landscape but mostly this night runs past anonymously in the French countryside; among these mountains even the train must seem to anyone who hears it merely a noise that is quickly lost in the silence. Now I am glad to have left. The moment I heard we had succeeded in avoiding the closure of the department for another four years I thought: I am going to Italy. But it was a sigh of relief at the end of those seven tremendous months rather than a decision; then the day for departure came too fast. Last night neither Julia nor I were able to sleep; it has become difficult to leave.

It still doesn't seem true to me that we managed to get the better of the administration—the next four years in hospital now seem pleasingly long! Departments like ours, that have a psycho-therapeutic approach, are not favoured by this government, they call up too many memories of the sixties. Most psychiatrists treat mental disorders like organic illnesses, they hand out drugs and distance themselves from psychology, which is always a form of social assistance (a tabu word today). The last seven months, since we learned that they wanted to close us too, were hell; instead of working in hospital one seemed to be overseeing the death row of a prison, and meantime never-ending meetings with these new managers who now keep an eye on us like a secret police. The nightmare of the closure of the department had begun precisely in one of these meetings when Djaktar, who had just arrived to train with us, interrupted the report of the new administrator to say that basically we were a public service and our job was not to make profits but to look after the sick. The administrator adjusted his spectacles, smiled indulgently at the 'young Pakistani doctor who is a guest in our country' as he unfailingly called him from then on, rattled off some moralistic rubbish about people's capitalism with the same lazy arrogance with which the television trots it out every evening, then he went back to go over the accounts loudly as if to say: The reality is in these figures, if you wish we can also talk about your opinions. We listened to him in silence, Djaktar had said the only thing a doctor could say and with such frankness that now there did not remain many possibilities for compromise. At this point it was clear that any argument against the cuts would be another kind of discourse, that of humanitarianism: 'You are avoiding the knotty questions, gentlemen, the government is spending money it does not have, if we want to save the hospital we must make profits.' Thinking that at this point he ought to add a touch of ideology, the administrator allowed himself some more generalisations about the fate of the free world and the end of socialism in Great Britain, looking Djaktar straight in the eye he even said that it is important to find points of contact between the different grades working in the hospital and that he was grateful to the 'young Pakistani doctor who is a guest in our country' for having wished to contribute to the discussion with his personal impressions:

'What department do you work in?'

'With Dr Masini.'

'Another talent from abroad.'

We were all anxious at this point: to expect profits from the Archway hospital is like dedicating oneself to making a garden on a motorway. Would some rich hypochondriac prefer our cement hospital on a main road full of traffic to the private clinics in the country or to a famous doctor in some elegant district? Hypothetical profits apart, we were all waiting for the administrator to be clearer about the cuts which was what the meeting was really about. We seemed to be sitting at a game of Russian roulette, Djaktar had asked in the name of the department that they allow us to shoot ourselves before the others. The meeting closed without sentence being pronounced, but the very next week we received a laconic communication from the administrative board which announced that it was impossible to keep the department for lack of funds. We got to work at once: we wrote four thousand letters, to former patients, to the papers, to politicians, to all possible allies, sleeping something like twenty hours a week; we had interminable meetings with the unions and the administration until demagogy was coming out of our ears, but in the end we won! At least for the next four years and meantime let's hope the government falls.

We went to sit on the lawn in front of the little building that houses the department, at the far side of the hospital, along with the nurses, Djaktar and some patients, to celebrate with cans of beer, some terrible white wine and fruit juices. It was already hot, I lay on the grass and listened a little longer to how they chatted—Oonagh, the Irish nurse who is laughing, plump and soft, flirting with Djaktar, who will soon have finished his training and we hope to be able to keep him on a decent contract, that they won't put my mad people out on the street any more, the grass soft on my neck, the temperature mild and a sleep that arrives slowly from seven months ago and into which I at last collapse sighing happily: welcome back, my old tranquil life! Now that no one is taking it from me I can once more complain a bit about my work, like everyone else, and welcome summer evenings, and Julia, and everything peaceful, everything is as it was before this nightmare.

When I reopened my eyes it was dark, they had all gone away. Someone had thrown a jacket over me and in my drowsy state I had heard someone saying 'Shall we wake him?' and Djaktar replying 'No' and I thought 'Good'. The sky was full of stars, I looked for the

THE WAY BACK

Aquila, Cygnus, Cepheus, Cassiopeia. Almost the same sky as tonight's.

They are all still sleeping in the compartment. I look at the stars again, always the same over the whole northern hemisphere; whereas on earth a few hundred kilometres suffice to change people, trees, languages, ways of doing things. By dint of making diagnoses I sometimes end up by allowing myself to be lulled by the handful of things I know, I feel I can explain everything, then all I have to do is cross a frontier to feel myself entirely unprepared for the world that begins there. It only needs a few hours alone in the night, under a sky like this, to forget the things which for months seemed so important. When I think back to what little my mother left, to the nurses who couldn't bear her any longer in her last days, I am afraid to see the few memories I have of her disappear still faster. They go into a silence in which her whole life is nothing. Everything goes and we go in the same way, like trains and memories, without even the consolation of having understood where they go. One repeats things, one denies things, one wakes up and every day we are back at the beginning again. Then one day I too will be dead, and the silence of this future, the nothingness of that absence—so near—terrifies me. Even if for me the fear of death is above all horror at the banality of it, of the fact that to die is only to die, merely going into a state of nothing. Everyone wants to leave an object to someone because it can say: I was his, he was made that way. Instead, even before death cancels out places and moments, distraction comes along, forgetfulness, the regular flux of daily banalities, to cover the world with dust, to transform what was familiar into something strange, to make us feel that we have arrived in this world again by chance, tonight.

Now at least there is a train which is carrying me away. But that night, waking up on the lawn, I felt my life to be tied up with the next four years in hospital and far from me, destined for someone else, while I was left there bodiless, wandering under the stars. I had got up and was walking towards my department, a prisoner of my steps, as if everything in me desired another life and was forced instead to follow what I was doing; I had to link my thought to that place and to that moment but I did not succeed and hoped to meet someone who would ask me something and thus force me to pull myself together.

The duty sister came towards me, worried. Krystyna had once again created a fuss about going to bed.

Krystyna Smerz is a girl of nineteen of Polish origin. When she arrived she weighed sixty-five pounds. To begin with we fed her intravenously; as soon as possible we began the psychotherapy, both alone and with her family. Her father does not speak English at all, her mother keeps saying: 'Krystyna is well: when is she coming home?' Krystyna's illness is born from this: she has integrated herself rather well at school and in the district where they live, she is an English girl, of this city and of her time. But the Smerzs have always remained in the Polish community, tied to a morality, to traditions too remote from this country, they look back to their village, to the Second World War, they no longer make efforts to adapt, they don't even try to speak English any more. If Krystyna becomes an adult in this country her success will grow between her parents and her. The better she understands and makes herself understood by the English, the further she will be from them. Father and mother have worked seventy hours a week for their children, they are nice, gentle people but their affection is precisely the terrible blackmail Krystyna faces. Whatever they say (and say even with their silences) they merely repeat: So you are growing up? are you leaving us? Anorexia is Krystyna's answer.

The other day, after the session, the mother followed us into the corridor and said once again: 'Krystyna is well, sooner than hurt us she would kill herself!' Djaktar was touched and I had to reply: 'Our problem, Mrs Smerz, is that she almost succeeded.'

Sometimes it seems that her parents understand, that they are capable of helping her to construct an adult life without having to feel guilty about them; but at other times they again clutch at the sentimental banalities with which they do her violence: they recall how happy they were once when Krystyna was our good little girl, how she always helped mummy and how she loved daddy, and in my heart I wish she may not put on weight too hastily, if she does I shall have to send her home and in three months we are back at the beginning again. In certain attitudes of Mrs Smerz I seem to see my mother again with her awkward Italian, slow, packed with *zabka* and *ptasszyna* and other little incomprehensible pieces of Polish.

I had forgotten what *zabka* means. As I was driving down the hill to Archway so many words came to mind like this one of which I had forgotten the meaning. After so many years I thought again of my mother's last months in the San Giovanni hospital in Rome. The wards, the smells, and one evening I opened the small chest where I keep the few things she left me. There ought to have been a little Polish-Italian dictionary as well, but it had vanished. Instead I came across a photograph of a little girl in front of a villa, on the back there was written: Ania, 4/6/27. It is her, on her fourth birthday. Then there was the diary of her flight from Poland in '39 and a letter, the only one she ever wrote to me (she did not feel at ease when she wrote in Italian).

> Rome, 15.8.79
>
> Drogi moi Dawid,
> Congratulations on specialising in psychiatry.
> Ty yestes moy madrala! Signor Cavalieri has
> been very nice about pension, everything all
> right today. Thank you. At last I breathe. Want

to see you but don't come to London, too far.
Forgive me. But want so much to see you again.
Your success consoles my loneliness. You are
doing right thing. You must do what is best for
your life. This summer in Rome is getting very
hot. Too hot really. I ought to do so much but
don't feel like going out, in the street can't
breathe so much sun. So many things I ought
have done in life, one more doesn't matter. But
don't worry, *my Doctor*.

                    A very big hug, moi zabka
                              twoja mama.

There it is *zabka*. What does it mean? I had to go and pick up Julia who was singing Susanna, I turned on the water to have a bath but I had slipped away from what I was doing; once again I was carrying out my gestures automatically, as if someone else were doing them, the only thing I had in my head was that I was sorry not to remember what these Polish words meant. I had decided to ask the interpreter who helped us in the therapy sessions with Krystyna's parents to translate for me the words I did not know in the letter and at least some pages of the diary. While taking my bath I fell asleep and had a dream: I was walking with my mother in an ancient city, between broken, pink walls. She was trying to tell me something but there was no time, I was in too much of a hurry to go to another city and she came to the station with me. I had not wished to hear what she had to say to me and hoped to get to the train before she began to speak. At the end she looked at me, asking me with her eyes: 'Did you understand all the same?' I had not understood and went back to look for her in extremely long corridors, which were sometimes those of my department, sometimes those in San Giovanni; I heard her voice without being able to catch up with her, it was cold, and my train was about to leave.

I got to the theatre only for the last act, I found an assistant director who guided me through the corridors to the wings from which I was in time to hear Julia singing her aria. She was very good indeed. When the curtain came down and the curtain calls began she came and hugged me for a moment, she was excited and I sang softly in her ear *thou'llt break my heart, thou warbling bird*. For her it was a long road that led here, full of work. I knew this but could not be really close.

The curtain went up again and the stage was once more invaded by a cluster of lights and applause. Julia went back to the centre of the stage, an attendant handed her a bouquet of roses, flowers rained down from the gallery and, leaving Susanna behind her, she had already begun to walk again with her usual mysterious simplicity, frightened of the public.

They invited us to eat in a restaurant on the Thames; I was sitting opposite the conductor, a conceited

THE WAY BACK

Sassenach who talked to me at length about easy loans and cars. He had vague ideas about Italian opera, mistaken ones but ones that are unfortunately common in England, and every so often blundered into some gross errors about our political history. The singers on the other hand were nicer, they drank with gusto and in their conversation strange languages mingled, the Venetian Italian of Da Ponte, Boito's nineteenth-century version, phrases with odd constructions full of words that had been Italianised behind the scenes of all the theatres in the world. They told stories, stories about sex and journeys, like commercial travellers, and every so often I caught Julia's glance searching for mine. I hoped that the vulgarity of certain comments would not upset her, I found it rather amusing.

We got home in a good mood. I had forgotten my mother's papers on the bed, Julia was excited by her success, she kept on talking about the characters she would like to interpret in the future; she took up the photograph of the little girl in front of the villa and asked who it was but she got distracted right away and started to talk about the theatre again. We undressed, we washed and went to bed. Julia asked me again about that little girl. I had in my mind those words the meaning of which I could not remember, *zabka, madrala*, and while Julia was falling asleep I awoke from the lack of interest in which I had buried my mother, in my ignorance about her and her world. I stared into the dark and could not wait for Thursday to come, the day on which we had the sessions with the Smerz family, so as to ask the interpreter to translate that diary for me.

With Krystyna we had certainly made progress: her weight was almost back to normal and her parents had understood that there was a problem to solve; the other neurotic symptoms were also beginning to go away. We began to glimpse the end of the treatment; I had asked the interpreter what *zabka* meant. 'It is a term of affection—it means frog.' I had also asked her whether she could translate some pages from the Polish diary for me. In her too there was something that reminded me of my mother; when she came into my house and I took her coat I noticed that she moved her body in the same exact, measured way. I showed her the letter as well and asked her what *ty jestes moi madrala* meant.

'You are my brainy one.'

I found it difficult to talk to her, I had suddenly to translate from the Italian sentences which began with the formal mode of address, which make no sense in English, and I felt she would in any case have had difficulty in understanding me because she was Polish. It had not happened to me for years, after a few months in England Italian had withdrawn to somewhere inside me, it never interfered with my English.

The translator sat on a sofa with my mother's diary and began to read while I made coffee in the kitchen. Placing the tray on the little table I sat opposite her. She smoothed her skirt with one hand, smiled at me and went on reading for more than an hour. At the end she took off her spectacles and sighed: 'It is the story of so many Poles in those years. Your mother is very observant and writes well even if sometimes she feels a bit like Greta Garbo. How old was she in 1939?'

'Sixteen.'

'Right! So, doctor, you know that your grandfather was in the textile business and had got an important commission from the government. Your mother writes that as she saw it he was giving money to a certain Grabowski, an official in the Ministry of War. This gentleman must have had a weakness for young girls, on the twentieth of June your mother notes: *I came down to table today with one of mother's dresses and wearing No 5 lipstick. Grabowski got drunk and Papa was very angry. Mrs Grabowski stuffed herself with sweets as usual, her stomach will get even bigger. Grabowski said he wanted to see me dance and I put on an American record of Aunt Sara's, I danced, then Grabowski offered me a cigarette and I lit it in front of everyone. Papa asked me to follow him into the study, he shut the door and gave me a slap. It didn't hurt much.*

'On the following days too there is a kind of girlish thoughtlessness, they really couldn't imagine that Germany would invade like that, from one moment to the next. But your grandfather was following the political scene closely, I think, because he did not believe in the optimism of the communiqués, which praised the resistance of the Polish army, and he managed to anticipate the flight of the government. Listen to this—it is the sixth of September: *Yesterday morning Papa told me to put on a woman's dress, the lipstick and high-heeled shoes. He was very sad. We took the sports car (the last one left, they have confiscated all the others) and went to Warsaw to see Grabowski in his office. Papa began to talk about business. I wanted to get out and take a walk in the city, eat an ice-cream, it was already late and papa kept on repeating the same things.*

Grabowski was impatient too. Papa was very slow, as if he were waiting for something to happen. The telephone rang and Grabowski made a signal for us to leave the room but Papa caught my arm to make me stay seated. I did not understand, it was very rude. Grabowski put down the 'phone, he was extremely angry, then Papa got up and, as if nothing had happened, said that unfortunately he was in a hurry, he had to meet someone and if Grabowski didn't mind I would stay in the office for a little. Grabowski banged the table with both fists and said: "Goldman, don't go too far!" Then Papa offered me a cigarette. I understood less and less. He made me light up and asked me to open the window. I got up and heard him suddenly say: "I really have to rush off, thank you, Grabowski." He seemed to be saying goodbye but I did not manage to turn round and look at him because the window wouldn't open. I felt Grabowski's eyes on me like when in our house he begins to smoke Cuban cigars and drink too much slivovitz and then wants me to dance even if he knows that Papa gets angry. There was something wrong with the handle of the window, I was using both hands and the smoke was getting in my eyes, my shoes were hurting me and the skirt was too tight. My eyes were watering because of the smoke and I was ashamed to turn round, I still felt Grabowski's eyes on me and I must have been very ugly because the make-up had run. At last that damned window opened but the handle remained in my hand. I turned round and saw Papa standing near the door with his head held down. I ran up to him and pulled at his arm. "When are you coming back?" The arm was so lifeless that the sleeve seemed empty, he took leave of Grabowski with a strange smile. "When are you coming back?" I asked him again, he looked at me for an instant, his eyes were shining and he whispered to me: "ratevè sich." These two words are not Polish, perhaps they are Yiddish. No sooner had Papa gone out of the door than a great hubbub started, people arrived, ladies, children. And Grabowski's wife who looked askance at me. We left before dawn.

'So she escaped from Warsaw with the government. On the eighth she notes again: *Better news says they have broken through the German front at Kielce. France has taken the Ruhr and the Saar.* Vain hopes. They travel east at night because during the day the roads are bombed. The convoy disintegrates, there isn't petrol for everybody and so some people go to look for horses from the peasants to pull the cars. On the ninth she writes: *They say Warsaw has fallen.* On the fourteenth: *We passed Marshal Smygly and the government.* So from now on it must be everyone for themselves and all are fleeing. At a certain point they meet a caravan of refugees, people escaping from the opposite direction, from the east to the west. They have carts full of household goods, furniture, children. Someone asks what they are escaping from and the others reply that the Russians have invaded from the other direction. So your mother's group also changes direction, they go south towards

Romania. Your mother, doctor, became a woman in a few days.'

The interpreter looked at me, she had stopped speaking.

'What can I do to thank you?'

'Nothing actually, doctor, it was a pleasure to read these pages. My father was an anti-Nazi writer who tried to flee along the same road but too late; he never succeeded in reaching Romania, they took him and he died in Treblinka. But your grandfather was very clear who would survive.'

'He died in Treblinka too. My mother was the only one of the family to survive.'

I continued to think about this story almost regularly from that day on. Was it possible that my mother had never told it to me? and yet something I did know, probably she had spoken about it in the years when I didn't listen to her, it was part of that landscape of the war years, which I found confused—years when of course she had also been there and many, many others with stories like that. Her flight, the grandparents, Treblinka, her generation, had been absorbed by me from her person, they were her, her pain. If at home I repeated some of the ideas I had heard in school, in assembly, or that you could read in the papers, she fell silent, she was against *communism which took everything from us*, or else she changed the subject. I became stubborn and began to hold real political meetings: I explained the necessary reforms, how we would eliminate the conveyor belt and school, my own proposals for international politics and, given the kinds of resistance that would inevitably be offered, the necessity of revolution. Wisely she didn't listen, so to provoke her I ended up talking about refugees, all those people who have only prison, tyranny or hunger behind them, and who end up cleaning the houses of the rich or *being concierges like you*. Then she shouted at me that the world is an accursed place and that I have no idea what these tens of thousand lire she brings home at the end of a day's work mean. She began to weep, she had had no luck with men or with money. She had been rich as a girl and poor for the rest of her life, everything had been a struggle, to earn one's living in a foreign country, to bring me up trying to protect me from a world even she did not fully understand. All her life she re-used every piece of cloth as if the war were not over and thus, scrimping on everything, she helped me to get through university. 'We are Italians now,' she said to me, 'this country has given us something to live on. You are Italian and must behave well, moi Dawid, just imagine what humiliation your grandfather Daniel...'

When she got to this point I could not listen to her any longer; her suffering was enormous, faced by her pain, my protests had to give way as if hers were *the* pain in the world. I tried to avoid that story, I felt that basically she was asking me for something in return—something I could not give her. Thus, as soon as I had a life of my own, I began to tease her a bit so as not to have to listen repeatedly to stories about the war. Sometimes she smiled, at other times she was upset and began to weep again, holding me tied to that knot of tenderness and violence of which our bond was made. As the years passed she was unable—with me at least—to do anything other than suffer and console herself and I was always the cause of her anxieties and the source of her comfort. I also have happy memories of her when I was a child. Then she was able to cast off her mourning, or perhaps she still had the hope of a different life from the one she lived. For example when she helped me with my lessons, I must have been seven or eight, I imitated her mistakes in grammar and she began to speak to me very rapidly in Polish and to suffocate me with kisses and hugs. If I didn't want to study on the other hand she would say: 'So you don't want to become Dr Masini?' How she kept on at me! Today I no longer know whether to laugh or cry with that Dr in front of my name. *Your success consoles my solitude.* Who knows, perhaps I worked so much only to provide myself with a reason for leaving her, to protect myself from her disappointment, the pain that I read in her face, a pain which had brought me into the world and for which I would have liked to have repaid her and faced by which, however, I felt impotent. So I always felt pity for her fate and fear that this pity might end up by paralysing my life, making it merely a continuation of her unhappiness, an echo of her suffering. I had to be born, and I did not even know this when I left.

She would have liked to see me rich, married, with

children, and then perhaps from my children and the children of their children she would have wanted the same and so on for ever and ever, to give back to their progenitors what we cost, what was taken from them and never given back. I looked at other women and was already thinking that I could not give her much more. She would not like Julia, she would not like that she had been married, that she earns more than me, that she doesn't want children. Perhaps she never really liked me either. She said I was everything, and I have always felt that this meant also being everything I wasn't.

For some minutes I have been noticing the outline of the landscape again. Along the line of the horizon, to the east, a strip of light has found its way between the mountains and the night. The rocking of the train which led me to think in my half-waking state now wakes me slowly from my thoughts. I begin to look at things again. I still miss my mother today but once more I have stopped thinking about her. For some time, while I was making supper for Julia and myself I surprised myself asking my mother for forgiveness. I always knew so little about her and when I realised that one day she would be dead and would no longer be able to tell me anything it was too late, she was already in hospital, she was suffering a lot and didn't want to talk any more. I did not know if the interpreter was right when she said that as a girl she felt like Greta Garbo, if this Grabowski was really a swine who had made her unhappy or if she had imagined it, if other men (and which ones?) had hurt her, I did not even know who Signor Masini was. She said he had died of a tumour, but I never saw anything of his, not even a photo; knowing her, it could even be a name she had invented to get a residence permit. I wanted to stop asking myself these questions and to get out of this chain of thought; my life now asked for other things, Julia was with me, and Krystyna who had to learn not to be afraid to grow up. Instead I tried to find someone who knew Yiddish and again it was our interpreter who found me the telephone number of a friend of hers who could help me.

'Good evening, I am a friend of Mrs Mitzkievic, she tells me that you could help me with two Yiddish words which I want translated. Do you know what *ratevè sich* means?'

'Save yourself.'

II

In Bologna I got out of the train with my suitcase, convinced I had to change trains, I went to the bar and when I heard the departure announcement ran back to the platform in time only to see the last coach with its fine sign *Rome* shoot past under my nose and to watch the bits of paper pirouetting on the rails in the draught. The next fast train is in an hour. I sat in the waiting-room; in front of me I have the memorial tablet for the massacre of the second of August nineteen eighty, I read the names of the dead, then an article I found in the train and meantime look at the people in the room. I think of someone who on that second of August had missed a connection, maybe someone like me who has spent some hellish months shut up in an office writing letters and having meetings and who finally has got a weight off his chest and wants to disappear for a few days. His wife is at the seaside with his son and his in-laws; he doesn't feel like plunging immediately into the family circle, he'd like to draw breath and take off somewhere, go and look up an old friend or maybe end up in a city he doesn't know. Just for a few days, to empty his head. Perhaps it would be better to take the next train instead: he will arrive very late and tomorrow he'll go to the beach even if he doesn't like the sea, that way at least he won't have to lie. Even he doesn't know what he will do in the end, but in any case he ought to 'phone now to warn them that he has missed the connection. In the best of cases he has an hour to kill; he wanders about the station phlegmatically, and he doesn't dislike the chaos that is going on, it is the first weekend in August, many students who have taken their final exams, many workers, the usual foreigners, there's a holiday feeling. He is wearing a suit bought in a department store which protects him from his colleagues at the board meetings, a suit exactly like theirs which doesn't give much idea of what he is like, of what colours please him, of his body, a suit that makes him feel safe at work but still makes him a little uncomfortable when he orders a coffee at the bar; in his free time he is more elegant and easy-going, but today he doesn't mind being dressed like this, after all it is fitting: he has been a worker, has been a student, sometimes he has also been a foreigner, has been on holiday and today is as he is, like his light-coloured suit, and he likes to belong among that infinite number of other people with whom he queues at the ticket-offices in the stations, who take trains, who watch football matches, who crowd the beaches and queue on the autostradas. Even the telephone calls he must make now, the embarrassment at the little lie he'd like to tell, the indecision about what is best at this moment, whether to go straight to the sea or to take a few days' holiday from the family, his moderate and often contradictory love for his wife seem to him things so sacrosanct and ordinary that he has no desire to take decisions; for this reason too he moves about calmly waiting for something to happen. For people like him, always too intent on pursuing goals, it is important to find these pauses, to be able to look at the world and listen to its messages. He notices he is talking to himself as if in a board meeting, as if he had to convince someone else and this makes him laugh to himself for a moment. After all this too is right, he thinks to himself once more, like the suit. But there is no one at home and he goes back to sit in the waiting-room. It is very hot, they will certainly still all be on the beach, he doesn't remember what they told him nor what he said in his last call nor when it was. Perhaps they aren't even expecting him today, but it is better to give a sign of life, I wouldn't like them to call the office and be worried. They never write anything in these magazines, half of it is advertisements, and even the articles are nothing but advertisements. He looks round the room: two English boys have come in in shorts and T-shirts almost buried under huge packs and have sat down in the shade at the back of the room. One of them is reading the usual *Europe on Five Dollars a Day*, the other a vocabulary of basic Italian. A small girl has made a little bed on a seat for her doll and is cooking puddings, cakes, wakes it up, sends it to sleep, puts it back in bed, takes it with her on fabulous journeys on imaginary trains and planes and cars. An elderly couple walk very slowly through the waiting-room, both have glasses with very thick lenses. In summer old people seem even more fragile, more vulnerable, perhaps because of the heat; but what beautiful, dignified elegance! He—on the second of August, at two in the afternoon—has a tie knotted as if he had to meet the President of the Republic, she actually has a little hat. To be wearing his light-coloured suit from one of the department stores now seems to him still more right and instinctively he adjusts the knot of his tie out of solidarity with the old man. Both are eighty at least, she has his arm and guides him, but she is also used to making sure that she is protected and makes him walk a few inches in front of her. Every so often, when he raises his eyes from his magazine, this person whoever he is, finds them again, still making their journey to the other end of the waiting-room, and wonders at their patience and their constancy. Why don't they sit down nearer the door without having to make that journey? At last they have arrived; they too have a place in a corner in the shade away from the draughts, they are still arm-in-arm, a little frightened, too shortsighted to read, too intimate to exchange a couple of words just to pass the time. Then there is an extremely elegant and very beautiful girl, who is reading the same magazine as he is. She has a light coloured linen suit, bare legs, moccasins of soft leather, smooth hair, recently cut, very fine features. Every time he looks at her he wonders whether he can speak to her about some article in the magazine, looks at his watch, thinks it is time to ring his wife. Passing close to her he brushes against her with all his thoughts but she keeps her eyes fixed on the magazine. She can't find these advertisements so interesting! There is a bit of a queue at the telephone and crowds in the hall, at the tobacconists, at the bar. So many mothers, so many children, grandparents and grandchildren, men and women on their own. His wife isn't back from the beach this time either but soon, he thinks, looking at his watch again, he'll at least find his in-laws at home, it's almost two and they have their habits, they don't miss a meal for a little sun. In fact it is almost better if he gets his mother-in-law rather than his wife, he can lie to her without any hesitation in his voice, he doesn't have to explain to her what he's up to, he will leave a short message that can't be questioned: 'I can't be home before Tuesday, I don't have many tokens for the 'phone, ciao.' He goes back into the waiting-room and takes a long way round to get back to his place, he passes close to the old people, the English boys, the little girl and her doll, and sits down once more opposite the beautiful woman. He takes up the magazine again but does not read anything, he turns the pages and looks at the woman, he wonders how old she might be, what she might be called, what he could say to her. Will she be married? and does she work? At a certain point she will take a train, that is certain, and after all what other train could he take? He has made up his mind, he will say he has still two days of hell and that he will be back as soon as possible. He looks at his watch, gets up, passes close to her and this time she raises her eyes from her magazine, she looks at him thoughtfully, with amusement, then turns them back to the magazine, shaking her head slightly and smiling. He makes his way towards the main hall with a swagger, he tosses his telephone token in the air and catches it again in flight, he has completely forgotten whom he is going to call and is thinking only about what the next move can be with the beautiful stranger. He will sit down near her, but not too near, and will say something to her. Better not to think about it beforehand, he must neither push nor resist, these encounters only work when one follows one's inspiration—so enough plans. He follows the token as it spins through the air and, catching it again, he feels almost happy, certainly happier than one usually feels when one misses a connection in Bologna in August.

The blast hurls him against the panels with the timetables. For a few seconds there is silence, then the first shrieks. Now the heat is full of smoke, the bomb has torn open the wall of the waiting-room and through the gap one sees the sky above the dust. Help arrives, they dig in the ruins, begin to carry away dead and wounded. Among the stones a telephone token, the head of a doll, a pair of glasses, a moccasin of soft leather. The ambulances arrive in dozens, the bodies, covered by a sheet, will have been lined up in the square for the time being and as I look at the people in the waiting-room today and the names on this tablet I still do not know what separates us from them.

the nest and the farmyard

The train has stopped on a bridge on the outskirts of a city—it must be Florence. Below us a group of children just out of school is waiting for a bus. One of them, a thickset swarthy boy, is holding forth, telling of some adventure. His companions listen to him but don't allow themselves to be taken in; he might just be telling a story he has made up to make himself important. Then they ask him tricky questions, underline his exaggerations, repeat them to him, send him up for the romantic passages and his affected tone of voice, trying in this way to unmask the origin of his stories which, according to them, lies in some film and not in reality. The thickset boy interjects 'I swear' by this and that in order to defend his own version: then suddenly, perhaps irritated by the mocking air of another lanky boy who keeps on laughing, he adopts a knowing tone, a challenging one, as if it didn't matter to him whether they believed him or not, in any case that was how things really happened and to tell them the story again is something he can do without. At this point some of the group humbly submit, ask him more polite questions, invite him to go on; but the lanky one who led the counterpoint (terribly thin, he has trousers that come halfway down his shins) wanders round the group, kicking an empty Coca-Cola can. Perhaps he is jealous or else is simply fed up because the swarthy boy has begun to talk slowly, dug in in an unassailable position—of things that actually happened—as if he were God. He cannot bear it that his comrade demands to be believed literally, as if he didn't exaggerate or play things down, that he is pretending not to be part of that story and wants to impose the naked evidence of a reality no one has witnessed. As if he too wouldn't like to be a famous football player? or the actor on the poster that dominates their street corner with a smashing blonde leaning on his shoulder and another, perhaps the same one but maybe actually another, emerging from the dark in a cone of light in a very tight dress slashed at the leg, she too probably in love with him, at least to judge by the indifference with which he holds the cigarette in his lips? And isn't he there instead, like all of them, waiting half an hour for a bus after a day in school, almost certainly with the immediate prospect of a plate of soup?

But at this point it is no longer possible to object—that is something the lanky boy has understood: the little sheriff would have an answer to everything and however crazy it might be would impose it on the group, which would accept it, not because it believes it but because the swarthy boy perhaps has a toy motor racing track or fireworks and if you want to stay with the others, to take part in their games, you have to believe or pretend to believe these stories.

Is the swarthy boy the gang leader? I don't think so—the gang leader doesn't need to tell stories, everyone knows them already, they are the jargon, the essence and the reason for the gang itself which is, in fact, called Achille's, Hector's, Fernando's or Nicola's gang. The leader's stories are told only on the fringes of the group by rank-and-file members to new recruits in order to teach the rules, and to remind them of the existence of a not too distant authority that presides over the way things are. In this way the ordinary members become chiefs of a sort, that is to say, they place themselves between the new recruit and an abstract power, make themselves interpreters; and that is how the thickset boy keeps hold of them; he takes on the mannerisms of the cinema, by which they are in any case all attracted, claims to be closer to the world from which these attitudes come (America, bandits, soldiers, women, cars). Perhaps the real gang leader is actually the lanky one who, dethroned for the moment, is present at the birth by parthenogenesis of a new group; tomorrow they will be different from us, will be them, the others, and we will say that we were always different. Each group will be able to become a mafia organisation, a literary review, the political tendency in a party, or an armed band. The little boss of whatever it is who has agreed to make of his history the story shared by the group (from now on every fragment of his life, from the colour of his socks to his sexual habits, will be noted by friends and enemies intent on expanding or restricting the territory of that gang, which means of that discourse), will he ever be anything other than some sort of boss? He will soon learn that it is better for everybody if he is silent: the true discourse, in fact, is that produced by those who meet through him; were it not for that web of speculations, expectations, fears about him, he would be like the others. What will he do when, with the years and the growing biographical tangle, the story-telling boss at the bus stop discovers that he isn't the boss of the political discourses, not the strongest player at football or that he doesn't understand music? When, having become head of the class, of the school, of the Catholic or Communist students, power will begin to become a thing in itself, the only thing in the world, and the world over which he exercises that power, something so vast and perverse that at any moment it might rebel against him, demand his public humiliation, the unmasking of the lies on which he has constructed his authority? Down there, in the world he wanted to dominate, people go to work, play at cards and fall in love, can turn off one road and take another. If someone plays at cards with him you wonder what that person is going to ask him for, if someone loves him you think that person is a careerist. He cannot let go, get out of the circle, he is everything in the opinion of others, he is the opinion of others. It is those invisible others whose consensus he tried to win who have brought him here, to be what he is. Do the lanky boy and the swarthy one know this? No, they don't even know how complicated it will be to remain the head of this little group of boys when they encounter women and they all find themselves being alloted a new position by their verdicts. Maybe precisely the one who never wanted to be a chief has remained master of his own life, or, something that cannot be foreseen (under the infantile rules of power), he has guessed at a certain point that happiness is on another plane, elsewhere. For the time being, in their passionate arguments, they are one and all aiming high as if they were shooting at a street lamp with a catapult, they fire off bigger and bigger, more and more incredible shots. And high means more, better, higher than the others. They change their minds every day about what more, better, or higher than the others means. They think it is something you can possess, wealth, fame or strength. But each of these things ends up by being only itself, one is rich, famous or strong, so what? Only obstinacy can make him persevere with what makes him daily more lonely. He missed the group, his friends, because what drove him more, higher and better than they was not some thing but was them in fact, the others, the world, and that you cannot possess, you are in the world and you meet the others there outside yourself, in what you share with them. But in the meantime the bus has arrived and carried my boys away.

But my train remains standing for a long time and the growing shins of the lanky one buzz in my head like the thread of a newly rediscovered discourse. What will happen if the swarthy, thickset one, Livio, does not succeed in becoming the head of anything? The lanky one is called Davide, and now he is listening to him along with the others; he knows perfectly well that if he too submitted Livio would have got the whole class in his pocket. Livio knows this too and decides to invite Davide home.

To get to Livio's house on the Gianicolo you have to cross the park. Davide, who when he isn't at school is with the boys from his street, tells his mother he is going to do his lessons with a classmate who lives on the other side of the park where there are small villas, and she insists that he puts on a clean shirt. So Davide leaves home, dressed up, his hair parted, in the newest trousers his mother bought him six months ago which show his shins. His mother had actually suggested short trousers, cast off a year ago, and Davide told her she was 'immoral', he has heard the word on the radio, pronounced emphatically, he has guessed its weight but doesn't yet know what it means: he looks at his mother, trying to guess from her reaction something of the meaning of the word, but she did not hear it or perhaps understood something else. Davide does not insist and the word remains a mystery to him.

His mother's attention to his looks have made him uncomfortable, he is afraid of meeting his school friends got up in this way and her comments like 'look what a pretty boy you would be if you combed your fringe', or 'do you want them to think you've no one to look after you?' still linger in his ears. He feels that he is not alone even when he is walking through the park, he has once more become his mother's little boy, the cause of her worries and satisfactions. The shirt, those words, the thoughts with which he protests against her tighten his collar; he touches the top button, thrusts his neck forward like a dog on the leash, finally he recognises the boys from his street playing football on a patch of grass, he undoes that damned button, runs among them, finishes the match, saying at first that he mustn't get dirty and then, after the first stain, happy and swift of foot, he sweats, takes up his books again and runs towards the gate thinking of the goal he has scored. The dog is loose, at least for a few hours.

Livio's little villa is halfway down a long street with few houses and big plane trees. Davide rings the bell under the big brass plate that has written on it in an elegant hand the name of his schoolmate: *Cavalieri*. The gate clicks open and at the same time a big Alsatian arrives barking. Livio is on the stairs a few steps away and says to him smiling: 'Come in, he won't touch you.' Davide doesn't want to appear cowardly and comes forward, allowing the big animal to sniff at his hands with its damp nose. There is a lot of white gravel on the path through the flower-beds and Davide realises what a terrible state the school playground must be in; there nothing is left but a few miserable little stones in the dust but the ball bounces better. But then the tarred courtyards, like that of his block of flats, or the entrances to the garages, always crowded with small boys with skinned knees, covered with patches of oil and with people who look out and shout not to make such a din, are simply not of the same species as this garden. They have only one thing in common—the sky overhead. Davide has never seen a house like this, Livio leads him in. It is a princely house, pictures everywhere, some as big as a whole wall in his own house, there is even an empty suit of armour and a staircase that goes up through inaccessible floors where there are bedrooms and other rooms and who knows what else, perhaps someone famous. And handles of shining bronze, a banister of smooth brown wood, a statue in a niche and above all moquette. For Davide stairs are always dirty, with a woman bending down to clean them and people disappearing into their remote closed rooms; they are sawdust, the war between the smell of the cleaning materials and that of the cats. But here they are impeccably clean, shining, discreet, reserved for Livio's light steps and those of his family. Davide and Livio go down different stairs, not as beautiful as those at the entrance but wide, these too with moquette, and while they are chatting about what they have to do for the next day, about their teacher and their classmates, Davide sits down. Even Livio's chat seems precious, entirely natural in the way he uses words as mysterious and difficult as moquette. Davide, who is furtively stroking a step with the back of his hand and savouring it, would like to ask him what immoral means but it would be too explicit a confession of inferiority. So he asks: 'Do you think moquette is immoral?' Livio is not to be outdone and answers without hesitation: 'Certainly!'

They are in the playroom which isn't even Livio's bedroom, he sleeps upstairs with the other gods; it is only the room for his toys. He has so many, thinks Davide, that he actually needs a different room to keep them in! While they were playing and later, when they were doing their Latin and French exercises, Davide listened to the coming and going of footsteps on the floor above. In his block of flats too there is a continual to-ing and fro-ing of people and to check who is coming in is a conditioned reflex for Davide; they knock on the glass, to ask if there is a registered letter, or else where does Gallo, Caparrotti, Barbafiera, live. Third floor, number twelve. He watches them climb up the stairs along the dirty walls where each week the war of smells is renewed.

Every so often Livio is called upstairs to greet some guest and Davide hears exclamations of 'what a good-looking boy, how he has grown!' and then everyone laughs with seductive voices. But Livio comes back to play with him. Then he says he's hungry and they go upstairs slipping between the coats in a little room and into a kitchen where everything is modern. The maids are dressed in black with a little white apron and a frill on their heads, they come and go from the rooms with trays full of sweets and drinks. Livio and Davide drink cups of hot chocolate and *buchteln*, sweet, hot, covered with cream prepared by one of the maids who is Austrian. She really is Austrian! thinks Davide, looking at her and by now used to accepting the novelties of this house uncritically, 'We have to speak a different language every day,' Livio explains, 'that is why my father always takes on foreign maids, like at Anna Karenina's'. 'Who is Anna Karenina?' 'A Russian friend of Mamma's who has written a book.'

How easy everything is in this world! the china cups! the designs on the tiles! Livio's cashmere jumper! how clean and nice his friend is who has invited him into this house and stays with him, though he has only to appear elsewhere for one to hear so many voices saying 'Come here, handsome young man' and 'Do you remember me?' The Austrian maid shouts something at Livio, who is cleaning icing sugar from his jumper and even the shout in Austrian seems magnificent to Davide. From the other rooms which the maids can enter thanks to the trays piled with sweets and chocolate, there come the notes of a piano, the scent of rich women, inviting chatter. Davide says to his friend that you could make a nice dress with the moquette, strong, red and immoral, and this time Livio looks at him in astonishment.

Through the kitchen a most beautiful woman has appeared, her lips painted carmine red, her eyes made longer by pencil, her cheeks and cheekbones shaded with pale blue and pink tints, a string of pearls round her neck and a tight black dress like the one worn by the actress in the poster, also with the split on the thigh through which you see a bit of leg. Davide has his mouth full and cannot go on eating: he has never seen such a beautiful woman, he would like to stroke her face and kiss her knees, he looks at her, bewitched, while she says to Livio, 'Have you finished your lessons?' Livio nods and the woman disappears. 'Is she your mother?' Livio nods again, his mouth full. These are unhappy months for Davide's body, his legs are growing longer and his trousers are always too short, women no longer comfort him with the same caresses that once absentmindedly came down from on high; now they look at him with suspicion. In these last months Davide has known a new solitude which is not being alone but longing for women's bodies, the bitter taste of an innocence that is over and of his body which has become a guilty thing. Sometimes he feels like howling his hunger on the anonymous stairs of the block of flats. Every morning a voice comes down from the fifth floor; it is the maid of the family which has by its bell the little plate 'Ing. Giulio Angeli', a girl from the Marche with black, black eyes and hair, who puts out the washing, beats the carpets, cleans the windows. When there is the afternoon shift at school Davide sits in the morning on the window sill of the bathroom with his chin on his knees and listens to her singing:

> A blessing on whoever made your eyes
> which have brought you so many lovers

or else:

> Just once I want to risk it
> I want to come into your room.

And he has fantasies about the two of them, together,

fleeing on a sailing boat across the seas or in a racing car
towards the mountains or perhaps on horseback, dressed
as Arabs, in the Sahara desert. What a longing to be a
man, to protect her from the perils of the world and all
those big people who talk among themselves! And now
his legs are stretching out and would like to go into her
room but his beard isn't growing yet and his voice
breaks between childhood and maturity. He knows she
is called Nerina, the brunette with her dark hair and
eyes. He has heard her speaking to his mother and once
to a man outside the main door. When he is unable to
sleep at night he thinks of killing himself he misses her
so much and he is tortured till the morning. He listens in
the dark, thinks he will never sleep again. Even when he
seems not to be thinking about her, his legs sticking out
of his trousers remind him of her throaty voice and he
tortures himself, wandering round the house like a beast
without a prey, opening the fridge, sitting on the bed
and getting up again. Until once more her voice comes
down from the Angeli's flat along with the damp smell
of the stairwell, and enters the twilight of his mood.
When a sock falls from the line into the courtyard
Davide gets up and takes it back to her! how his eyes fill
with dreams, with hypotheses, with plans on the way up
those stairs . . . perhaps as she opens the door she will say
she loves him, will embrace him, will show him her
suitcase already packed in the hall and will ask him
gasping: Where is the sailing boat? where is the racing
car? where is the horse? Can he at this point hand her
the engineer's damp sock he has picked up in the

courtyard? Or let's be realistic: My dear Davide, forgive my forwardness but the engineer is always after me, I must ask for your protection and, while we're at it, tell you that it is for you alone that I sing hoping you hear me: let's get married!

Davide rings the bell, clutching that sock as if it were the last unbroken topmast of his sailing boat caught in a storm, the wind of his fantasy drives him towards the open sea, wrenches him from his hold: he will not ask her anything about her past, he will refrain from polite exchanges, he will hold out his hand to her and will tell her frankly: I love you, if you can't love me tell me at once so that I can throw myself down there. Instead she opens the door with a bundle of sheets in her hand, her feet in old slippers, her hair in disorder and says: 'Thank you, Davide, tell your Mum that if she doesn't mind I'll see the gate is shut myself tonight because last night I had to knock. Well then? what are you looking at?'

Can he talk to Livio about Nerina? It is the first time that it has occurred to both of them that the other is a friend and it feels as if each had to tell the other rather special things, to respect and like him. Livio has already told him that his father is called Carlo and is a judge, then that he has a big brother of nineteen called Fabio who has a two-seater sports car, and that he has a sister of sixteen called Adriana, still more beautiful than his mother, but this seems a bit too much for Davide and he has already decided that he won't like her.

Evening comes. Davide doesn't want to leave and someone says to him: 'But isn't your mother waiting for you?' and he sees that the sad time for farewells has come, he says goodbye, collects his notebooks and slowly sets off home. Farewell, big dog with the damp nose, farewell walls full of pictures, farewell moquette and ciao Livio, it's off to the wars! He shuts the little gate behind him and is once more on the street. Here once more you run the risk of being run over by a car, of being absorbed by the confused throng of the pavements, of getting shouted at by the colonel on the fifth floor for making a row. The park is still open and Davide crosses it again. It is an evening rich in smells, the eucalyptus and the oleanders are in flower, the crickets and the frogs are calling the stars out of the dark one by one with their rhythmical song. His stomach full of *buchteln* and chocolate little Davide goes down the path and takes a short cut, he is dreaming of the lady with the painted face who is Livio's mother; he would already like to tell that he loves her although he has only seen her for an instant. He loves Nerina too, but for the moment this is not important. But he also loves the woman on the poster, whom he has never seen, not even in a film, so we can say that, all in all, in the case of Livio's mother we have already made a good deal of progress. In this way, dreaming a little and thinking a little, Davide submits to Livio; in fact he had already submitted when his mother changed his shirt and he didn't know whether he could undo the top button, when he rang the bell at the villa, when he had to show he wasn't afraid of the dog, when he wondered why Livio had invited him out of the millions of boys who play in the courtyards to drink the chocolate made by the Austrian maids. And he thanks his luck, his benefactor who had told him so much about his family, and that warm evening, the song of the animals in the park and the light that sweetens thoughts. Who knows, perhaps among Anna Karenina's languages there is Polish as well and his mother could be taken on by the judge, both of them could go and serve in that house. Dreaming he reaches the street door and just about makes out Nerina leaning against a lamp-post and a soldier talking to her.

When his mother opens the door for him Davide at once begins to tell his story: extraordinary things in the princely house, Austrian maids and Turkish decorations! bejewelled ladies, pictures, marble statues and stairs— you should see the stairs— with moquette! Incredible, there's the mother, the father, and brother with a car and their sister. Davide's mother laments that his shirt is dirty already; as she takes it off him he goes on telling his story, he says there is a friend called Anna Karenina who knows all the languages in the world, so that—he thinks—they can ask to go into service in the princely house. 'Mamma, we'll be very well off! Ask the judge. You know Polish, you can cook, sew, you can do everything, why don't you ask him?' His mother is standing in front of the kitchen sink and trying to wash out a grass stain on the elbow. 'It won't go away!' she complains, 'why didn't you take more care, your new shirt!' and goes into the bathroom. Davide follows her, 'Why not?' he insists. 'Why not! I'm not going to ask your friend's father to be his servant!' and she weeps, she dries her eyes with her apron and keeps on rubbing the elbow of the shirt, then she sits on the edge of the bath and lets her head be stroked by Davide, who would like to ask her forgiveness but doesn't know for what.

But Davide remains the only one who has submitted to Livio. Livio isn't good at lessons, he doesn't play football well, he doesn't manage to steal chewing gum from the tobacconist, and he doesn't make people laugh, he doesn't win the right to be the chief on the field of battle by some heroic act and he doesn't awaken a feeling of tenderness in his companions when he has a real weakness. Behind his laments there is some kind of power, they are all aware of it: he has whims, he is spoilt, used to getting what he wants in the world by means of the petulance of his feigned sufferings. There is only one road for him; he will have to take them all, one at a time, to his house, show each one of his companions these stairs climbing up there and the Austrian maid, hoping that they will all be intimidated and astonished like Davide; if not, he can try to get them into his father's or brother's cars, give them presents of toys and maybe let them peep through the keyhole at his sister taking a bath. What would Livio not do to win the approval of the others! He will have to repeat till he is sick of it how important his father's work is, how beautiful his mother is, how many privileges have magnanimously been granted to his family by history, by the President of the Republic and by God Almighty. Only in this way, buying them with cups of chocolate, can he hope to make them forget or at least keep quiet about how these privileges have rendered him proud. It is a superficial pride, an obvious one, an external arrogance for he himself is intimately aware of the instability of these privileges (will they be left to him?) but his friends are not much given to subtleties, so long as there is a race-track for toy cars they come. They are not interested in seeing whether Livio believes in his boasts or not, if that way of signalling the origin of his claim to power (his father, his family, traditions) is not rather a sign of his expectation, the fugitive nature of that power; they don't notice how in reality he asks them to attribute to all this a value he does not believe in and which, on the contrary, he has already become accustomed to deny. Like Davide, but for different reasons, he suffers from solitude. Davide wants women, Livio friends. Davide is quick to understand situations and to cope with them, his world is the street. Livio, on the other hand, has spent so many hours of interminable, excessively boring afternoons checking that everything is in order at home. He knows every corner, every hiding place, every scratch on the walls of the house and the garden. He also is perfectly aware of the effect his words produce, how people react to certain words, what others are saying at every moment, and he believes in nothing and no one. All his life he has been repeatedly told how lucky he is and he has repeated it to others but what does it mean? Why if he really is so lucky can a teacher in school tell him he is stupid? Why can he be punished? Why is he judged if he is the son of a judge? Why these interminable afternoons alone? Why do they dump in his room only fortunate boys like himself who bore him to death with their fortunes which are like his own and which he cares nothing for? And all the while, perhaps his classmates won't let him play against the second eleven! Up to now, in fact, his place in the team had been guaranteed because he was the only one to have a leather football but now they have made a collection and there is a class football, maybe they won't pick . . . and he couldn't blame them, it always ends with him getting locked into the usual ineffectual display of dribbling between the side line and the goal, that damned dribbling which he's no good at and which is an ecstasy of omnipotence. Not to speak of what people have to put up with when to this delirium are added the sermons, the justifications, the reproaches aimed at his comrades, the insults to the opponents, 'They won't pick me . . .' He goes over and over it in his mind every day until the day when he confesses his fear to Davide.

'Of course we'll pick you otherwise there won't be eleven of us,' but Davide's assurance doesn't flatter Livio enough; Davide sees this and decides to say a few unpopular words in favour of his friend during half-time. His submission now seems complete, although

Davide does not notice it—but what does Davide notice? the brashness with which he discovers the meaning of words after having misused them is his one real resource. At his back there is no world that must continue, he has no traditions. Davide is his own gang-leader and has to throw himself into things at any minute. He has nothing to lose and this makes things easier for him, it allows him to let himself be borne along by events far beyond what he had imagined. Thus the socks no longer fall by mistake on certain mornings from the fifth floor; he hasn't had to produce either cars or sailing-boats, he merely followed her along the corridor one morning with the sock in his hand, there was no one else in the house, they touched each other and now she really sings a certain song for him in the morning telling him to come upstairs. Nerina has a fiancé and you have to watch out for the lady of the house, Davide knows he has to keep his mouth shut; little by little among the piles of ironing he discovers some of her downy hair, he listens to her talk about her village, savours the first kisses and soon the impatient course of sex. 'Davide, you'll come tae see me in Cingoli one o' they days, won't you?'

When he is standing in the street Davide now really feels himself the master of the world: come on cars and ratty colonels, I'm not afraid of you! so he hasn't even noticed that Livio doesn't invite him any more. One afternoon he absent-mindedly joins his classmates who for some time have been summoned in bigger and bigger groups to the villa on the Gianicolo, stuffed with sweets and hot chocolate, amused with expensive toys. There is a miniature car racing-track and it is Livio, naturally, who decides who may hold the switch, exhibiting in this way his magnanimity and his favours. Davide for one reason or another is always left out: either he is disqualified or else it isn't his turn or he's no good at it. Davide thinks of Nerina, and those games, his classmates and their age he leaves absent-mindedly behind him with a feeling of relief. But at a certain moment he too finds himself with the switch in his hand, but Livio snatches it away from him at once saying furiously, 'It's my game!' Davide asks him, 'Why don't you want me to play?' Livio remains silent and looks at him: What's this, he thinks, hadn't you submitted to me? wasn't I the boss? and then what happened to you? why don't you tell me about that maid any more? you think you come back like this, when you feel like it? but he can't say any of this, that would be to grant Davide the freedom to answer back: You the boss? don't make me laugh... Or even to reply in some way when Livio knows perfectly well that there is no possible reply. He looks at him, he narrows his eyes with hatred, there must be something in Davide that can be blamed. In his ears he hears the voice of his mother who yesterday evening at table said that the Jews are more intelligent than other people; Livio has already learned that these pat remarks of his mother's are devoid of any feeling. So without knowing what these words are, Livio says to Davide: 'Because you are a Jew.'

To be a Jew has never meant anything to Davide, for a moment he wonders: So what? It is a word like so many others, still empty for him, he has never used it. But he is Jewish just as he is tall and has curly hair. He understands from his eyes and tone of voice that Livio is attacking him, so he jumps on top of him and they begin to hit each other. The scrap becomes general, punches, neck-holds, red ears, scratching wool, teeth clenched in strained cries of 'Do you give in?' Davide is immobilised, he hears them plotting a punishment, from outside the melee he hears the cries of Livio's mother: 'Stop it! stop it!' and then 'Carlo! Carlo!' The beloved, cool lady who once lightly touched their lives from her exalted sphere, checking that they had done their lessons, whether they wanted a snack, now descends to free him. But how shameful to allow oneself to be caught ruffled and sweating, with these boys pinning him down. Where the lady is concerned his thoughts, now that Nerina is weaning him away, are no longer directed in a general way towards the realisation of adventurous dreams but are in a virile way concrete. He looks at her leg, which he had once glimpsed through a split skirt, he would want her stretched out and naked beneath him, on the immoral moquette of the staircase (why not?) beautiful, cold and severe!

The judge's intervention at once re-establishes the submissive role of Livio, who lets go of Davide, and on Livio's orders that of the others who leap to their feet like a well-trained team. 'What happened?' asks the judge. Someone called Alfredo goes over the situation:

Davide is a damned bore, he has held on to the switch for the track all afternoon, he wouldn't let anyone else play and then we rebelled. 'Right, make peace now or the track will be put away,' the judge concluded brusquely. Davide continues to stare at the floor, he doesn't accept the explanation this boy Alfredo gives but he doesn't want to be sorry for himself. As far as he is concerned they can all go and hang themselves, he is going back to the street. And then it is Livio who has to contradict Alfredo; if he really wants to be the chief he must know how to do it. Signora Alberta asks: 'What's wrong with this boy?' and strokes Davide's head in an annoying way. To begin with Livio tries to hide behind the voices of the other boys, says only, 'It's true, it was him,' hoping that there will be no explanation and that they will all continue to be against Davide. But his parents, his comrades and Davide as well, want to hear his version and he finds himself speaking alone while the others listen: 'Davide is a traitor, he has no time for anyone any more. He always used to be here, I let him play with all my things . . .' The judge is waiting for Livio to explain why they were fighting, he looks his son in the eye and Livio at last repeats to his father: 'And then he's a Jew.' The judge becomes red in the face and gives his son a slap. Livio knew he was challenging his father but he was caught between two powers—that of his father over him but also his own claim to power over his companions. With his slap the judge condemned the words and punished his son but in an involuntary way he has confirmed Livio in the eyes of his companions. That slap which Livio took publicly, with childish but tenacious dignity, is already a martyrdom. 'Do you realise what you said?' the judge asks in a fury. 'Of course they don't realise!' his mother pleads, caressing the heads of Livio and Davide. Now it is all over, Livio apologises to Davide but that slap has redefined the world; from now on his speeches to his companions will begin with *we, our generation, unlike our fathers*.

Then comes lunch, prepared for the occasion with the help of Signora Alberta who is more and more prodigal with her fondling of Davide's head. For Signora Cavalieri antisemitism and, in more general terms, racism, hunger in the world, working-class conditions, Right and Left, are one immensely complicated business —beyond the words she sees neither things nor persons, and then all that matters to her is her family. If she meets a demonstration in the street she reacts with irritation: What's this—don't we pay taxes? Don't we go to Mass? Aren't we living in a time of progress? so what are these people protesting about? The judge rebukes her daily for her political naivety, but gently, basically she knows he likes her like that. Fabio is harsher, sometimes he makes her feel really stupid, but he is her son and it remains in the family. But now, through Livio's words, she feels the moral inertia in which she has lived comfortably with her youngest child has been betrayed to the outside world. She would like to say to Davide that she thinks the Jews are more intelligent than other people but isn't sure whether that is the right thing to say at this minute, so she strokes his head. There will be discussions at table, Fabio will level the usual accusations at her, then he will quarrel with his father and she hopes it will all blow over quickly leaving things as they are. She is well aware that the nest she has built for her youngest child is absurd, the world is harsher than this. She watches to see that he doesn't hurt himself, that he doesn't keep bad company, she doesn't want to stop sheltering him.

Davide has other fantasies about her, he is not flattered by the vagueness of her caresses and at a certain point he takes her hand and removes it from his head. She perhaps understands and no longer humiliates him with absent-minded caresses.

When they have eaten they are led to the judge's study—a room with walls of books and a strong smell of pipe tobacco. They sit on big leather armchairs, the judge walks thoughtfully up and down the library, every so often he takes out a volume, looks up the index, lays it on the table or puts it back on its shelf, takes another puff at the pipe and starts walking about again. 'Do you know what the Final Solution was?' he asks the little group of boys. Alfredo, right off, improvises a cheeky answer which is ignored; the judge continues to walk up and down thoughtfully, he talks about the war, shows them some photographs of himself with Carlo Levi and Eugenio Montale in Florence in 1945. It seems the boys don't know these gentlemen, and they know nothing about the war and in the end Signor Cavalieri gets angry: 'What the devil do they teach you in school?' But they talk, they begin to ask a few questions, then Fabio and Adriana, the judge's older children, arrive, and the discussion gets lively. Fabio accuses the Catholic church of being jointly responsible for antisemitism, he talks about a certain Cardinal Innitzer who welcomed Hitler in Vienna. The judge gets heated and goes and takes a small book from a case and reads the homily of Cardinal Elia Dalla Costa in Florence being tortured by the Fascist gangs. Adriana joins in too, she talks about Vietnam, China and Cuba. The judge retorts with something about Hungary and Fabio interrupts him, says this is an old trick to shut him up. The judge shakes his head and mutters: 'We'll see.' So the boys discover the world of discourses, a world that talks over their heads and which none of them can yet reach, full of unknown words. Davide would stay all night listening but Fabio takes him and the other two boys in his car to their part of the town on the other side of the park.

Many days pass: Davide likes Livio for an odd reason which probably would not please his friend: because Livio is not a real chief but it is his lot to be one because of a family tradition, and he is rather pathetic. He sees him having problems, aside from his whims there is no obstinacy, no energy from a powerful future, only a desperate weakness, the inability to persist with projects, to defend what he has, to profit from chances.

When his whims in the course of the years reveal themselves for what they are, demands for the sake of demanding, Livio will not have built up the means for survival. In his angry lamentation Livio does not aspire to an object that is denied him, rather he denies himself the possible objects of desire in a delirium of self-sufficiency. Rather than with the privileges of his social condition it is with a radical nihilism that he has subjected the world around him. He is afraid of nothing, he exposes himself to risks of all kinds, he defies his teachers and all authorities with insolent insubordination. He loves danger and is full of fear: it is precisely this fear that attracts him and attracts the others around him. He loves the darkness that is at work there in danger, his is already the love of death. Close to him everyone becomes prudent and curious, seduced by his sombre inwardness. He comes home alone to eat and sleep, his mother despairs and thus encourages him.

He went to see Davide and has been in the street with him, they played football in the garage, then Livio showed off in front of the other boys from the street; he climbed a lamp post, he got the ball back from the other side of the wall where there is a dog that is greatly feared, he blew a raspberry at the colonel who looked out and shouted. From that day on the boys in the street asked Davide for news of Livio. And Davide shares in the general admiration for his friend.

Giving way to the pressure of his wife, the judge now dedicates a morning a week to the re-education of his daredevil son and Davide is chosen to be the good schoolmate. At seven every Sunday the judge and Livio come by to pick him up in the car, they get out at Porta Portese for half-an-hour or so, the judge buys some old books and often gives one to Davide too saying: 'He is a splendid writer for someone of your age,' or else 'There, that way you will understand where the Greeks were in Rome at the fall of the Empire.'

During the week Davide reads them from beginning to end and next Sunday discusses them with the judge who gives him more. Afterwards they go to the Forum or to visit some church or museum. The judge jumps about on the stones of the temple of Castor and Pollux or on Caesar's altar like a boy, he follows Livio and Davide who are very skilled at getting under the netting protecting the excavations, he begs them not to touch anything, he quotes from memory long passages of Latin poetry and other mysterious things. For Livio these walks are painful; he never remembers exactly what his father explains. Davide on the other hand always knows it all, doesn't get the popes and emperors mixed up and has read four novels by Jack London, two by Stevenson and now it seems is reading a book of eight hundred pages. Livio knows that these hours are set aside by his extremely busy father for his re-education and sees clearly that the judge prefers to chat to Davide and so decides to learn by heart the list of the Roman emperors.

One Sunday morning after the usual little excursion to Porta Portese, they went to Ostia Antica. It is already winter, Davide is talking about a horrible

Father Pendola, who is in the book he is reading; Livio goes over his emperors in his head. They are sitting on the steps of the theatre, it is cold and they talk and talk... there is a little dog sniffing at all the pines in search of his love. Livio calls to it. Finally they fall silent, he must be quick so that they don't start again. He goes over to his father and standing in front of him he begins to recite the names of the Roman emperors. He has only got to Caligula when he has his first doubts but he goes on saying the names, stroking the little stray dog which is wagging its tail between his feet and at a certain point the list comes to an end. Has he forgotten anyone? he remembers that the last was Romulus Augustulus but is that them all? And then what happens? Are there centuries without emperors and without names? Who knows how many nice little dogs like this wandered about the Forum or on the steps of this theatre and no one has ever thought that it was worth while remembering their names!

The judge did not grasp right away why Livio should display himself by this shopping list; for an instant indeed he was ashamed that his son should want to be such a swot in front of his friend when there was no point. He was just about to say to him: 'Well done, Livio, we all know who the Roman emperors were.' But after the first blunders, seeing that Livio was gazing desperately up in search of names he did not know, he felt a painful sense of embarrassment; he wanted to stop him, with the gentlest of words, and instead he painfully followed the effort his son was making to pick up a thread that made no sense to him and how he corrected himself, adding even more terrible mistakes to his lapses of memory as if to Livio that Roman world they had been exploring together for some months, were remote, incomprehensible. What patience his son must have had all those Sundays if that world said so little to him, with what devotion he had listened to him spouting Latin. Now he had actually tried to memorise for him names which were as distant to him as those of a Chinese dynasty. The judge took Livio in his arms, held him tight and stroked his head and it was clear, or at least it was clear to Davide, that they would no longer spend Sunday morning in that way and with that embrace in which he was not included he said farewell to the judge who had given him many books and taught him so much.

Many years go by: Nerina has married her soldier and gone back to her village, school came to an end and then started again for a while, then it didn't start any more. In the tarred courtyards and the flower gardens so many people have dreamt and struggled to get out of their ghettoes and their nests; after them, others a few years later were already repeating that same world in a different way, taking the same paths which, gradually as the troubled mists in which they search for the future thin out, reveal that they are the roads of the world.

Other buses have passed, other boys have leapt on to

them. Slowly at last my train too moved off, soon we shall be in Florence. The boys remain boys while every day a train goes away from them pulling on the thread of memories, the longing for what was and is no longer, so much so that perhaps it never really was like that. A nostalgia which continually murmurs, secretly, under the veil of the passing hours, measuring the distance between what is and what is lacking. A nostalgia against which I have always fought trying to fill the gap with a gesture or a word but which—no sooner had I deluded myself that I had finally arrived somewhere—turned round to call me from a little window through which I saw the landscape run past and the world I had found lose itself once more.

*the angels lose
their feathers*

I

We can't sleep. Lying in bed we seek sleep but it doesn't come. Come down, angels, and take away our thoughts. Instead it is a bright night, some cars are passing in the distance in Holloway Road. The senses have been in play an infinite number of times, now our arms and legs ask for a truce. What time can it be? Julia isn't sleeping either, I know; every so often I glimpse in her eyes the rays of the moon, I know she is sad because tomorrow morning I am taking the train to Italy. 'Can't you sleep?' She shakes her head and says nothing. Come down angels. I shall come back, I think, why doesn't she believe me? At times it is like waking from sleep, but we haven't managed to sleep. I go over in my head once more the things I have put in my suitcase and tell myself I am sleepy, if I don't sleep soon I shall already be tired when I get on to the train and the journey is so long. 'Have you got the book you wanted to take to your friend?' 'Sleep, please.' Come down, angels, close our eyes. Shut Julia's who is weeping and thinks I won't come back, the train will come off the rails, or else *far away from me you will be happier—another woman from your own country, some beautiful Italian who can understand jokes unlike me—as you say in Italian—choose women and oxen from your own village* 'Stop it, Julia, go to sleep now.' You are there torturing yourself and not speaking. Always the same, you refuse to speak, torturing yourself with terrible suspicions, then suddenly you come out boldly, suddenly cross the frontiers, wish to be affable with everyone and to show me that 'There's nothing wrong with me, believe me.' I see you again when you took me to the Lammermuirs for the first time: you stood there not saying a word, excited because you were showing me your heather-covered hills, the icy, invisible murmurs of the wind, which also seem to tell legends, you looked at me anxiously, hoping I would understand the landscape of your first life. Or when you asked me to teach you your first expressions in my language and the desperate and ferocious look in your eyes with which you sniffed at all the women I had known before you to see whether they had been my lovers. Come down, angels, I know what is busy there in her silence, I know that when we embrace at the door tomorrow morning your eyes will be full of tears as if everything that is being hushed by our hug were to come back suddenly, bleeding, rent, to scream from the brink of the fire: 'Save me, in my solitude there is nothing but death and pain.'

I pray to silence with my insomnia, but who can answer me? Angels, divine fantasies, once you used to console these hours! How often, going up certain stairs with my heart in my mouth, I anticipated with you the intimacy of long imagined kisses! I watched you flying like swallows in spring, busy and mad in a new sky, anticipating every moment of my expectation, suggesting at every step a secret promise. You filled me with sweetness—she has called me! My sorrows are over! she has asked me to come so enough of these doubts, let us celebrate with marvellous, complete confidence. And how often have I seen you lower your wings because of a mouth that turns away and refuses a kiss, because of something cruel spoken with indifference, because of the vain hopes of my excitement. How often have I sought you, shaking my fist at the sky because of your deceptions. You were speaking of paradise while life went on atrociously, you were encouraging me to take a chance, whispering 'go on' maybe even to throw myself into unforeseeable circumstances, naked at the feet of her coldness, repeating my devotion, and stammering out in my embarrassment the misunderstanding in which I was sinking! Weep angels, on your deflated clouds, weep because once more I have deceived you: I thought she was showing a patch of blue in her absent-minded gestures, it seemed that her voice, which was friendly at last, was opening up on a sky to fly in, and instead it was night; 'Go away' she shouted, 'and don't look up any more, your angels are plucked hens, butcher's meat!' Keep on playing among the clouds where there are no sharp corners only imaginary softnesses, I slip along the walls and pavements with my eyes lowered. Stay there leaning on your lamentations, don't lose your wings, don't lean too far out over us mortals, who travel on trains, confused and crushed, go to work and pay the rent. Down here your words will be mocked, don't try to blow on a dying flame, don't jest at her funeral. Ask her 'Do you feel the wind?', say 'Look what stars!' and it won't even move a leaf in her garden. If in spite of this a cherub should take off from your highest ranks in a suicide attempt and spread his wings to come down here, until he kisses her on a cheek, in a sadly natural way she will destroy him in mid-air, almost as if he were a fly, and that cherub, lost in the void of a gesture that isn't even cruel, then kicks me out of my fantasy on to the empty stage of her discontented eyes. 'What on earth are you dreaming of, you idiot!' For me the world was dead if she were far away, and if suddenly the telephone rang in my waiting the choirs sang, the trumpets sounded, all the heavenly ranks rose to their feet in a paradise of Glorias and Hallelujahs.

Lower your trumpets up there in paradise, fold back your wings, it's a wrong number! How much and how long your flights have been deceiving me, fingers pointing to a distant horizon, to the hope of landfall. No more angels, no more fantasies, only this night when we cannot sleep and Julia, who has embraced my wingless shoulders. 'Your passport? have you got your passport?' And no angels but sad Cassandras in white robes pass before my eyes, they keep saying to her 'He's leaving soon' and she implores their procession to be silent. Do not make predictions, my dear companions. But she weeps and if I ask 'What's wrong?', what come from her mouth are meaningless phrases, a song of funeral flowers, she searches around for calm and whispers, 'Suppose you die?' My little goddess has lost her way.

'Life is confused, a disaster, don't leave, don't go, where is my peace?' I stroke her head, she knows it is a childish sob to beg a mortal for anything. 'It's getting better now,' she whispers, drying her cheeks and to prove it to me she opens her eyes wide and constructs a smile. I look at her and feel very far away.

'What are you thinking?' I ask her and it is already as if I were on the telephone, her life, her body compressed into a second, a phrase, a tone of voice, so as to pass along a copper wire and to arrive far beyond the things I have around me. Once again her breath catches in her throat, she hides her head between my arm and the pillow, she weeps to herself and then perhaps manages to sleep. Who said angels don't have tears? What a heedless lover you have ended up with! in these few moments lost between bouts of sleep instead of saying to you I am not going far, I shall be back soon, I have got lost following thoughts that sought other loves.

Now there is only Julia's breathing, shallow, regular. Perhaps she is sleeping at last. It is still night and the silence is heavy on my chest because of everything I haven't said. I hear distant sounds of passing traffic, like sleep that comes and goes. It is still a long time till I have got to get up, round the edges of the curtain I look for the gentle light that lifts the night from us. And the moment the air becomes less dark I shall look into the sky to see whether by any chance a feather is falling.

II

I went to watch the retreating rails from the last carriage and there came to my mind one of the parodies in the style of Leopardi with which I killed time when I was driving Potter's buses from London to Edinburgh.

> Mute road and silent song
> Of the biting wheel; and you who run
> Over the rugged asphalt in the night
> Potter's coach . . .

I had so many solitary hours to fill and even in my thoughts I did nothing but wander. I was very far from everything I would have wished for and I tried to forget it in every possible way. I had no friends up there, with a great effort I had specialised in psychiatry which at that moment seemed completely useless and instead was doing a heavy and ill-paid job. I wasn't sure whether to stay in England, to go back to Italy, to try another country. But I didn't really manage to think of these things, they were the set for a scene without actors; while I drove I caught glimpses of the conditions in which I found myself like painted back-cloths, against

THE WAY BACK

which in contrast memories, the images of fantasy, stood out much more real. I liked the night, those long hours alone, to feel myself far away, to think that I owed no one anything, that I could disappear without trace, without regrets. Every so often in order to overtake I interrupted my mental wanderings: change down, indicate, move out, change gear again, move in again, take care. The moment I found the road clear again I at once caught the thread of the last interrupted thought, commonplace things and tunes came back to run through each other like the thoughts and the road under your wheels, *while you run over the rough asphalt in the night, Potter's coach* and I gave myself over to the way the miles ran past as if my bus could never arrive.

The journey in fact lasted eight hours with a stop at Toddington and one at Carlisle: all in all, the pay was really bad, but I have never been any good at that kind of sum. It was the summer that Livio died. What with terrorism and heroin it seemed that my generation in Italy had been decimated: of my schoolmates half were dead or had ended up in prison.

The best thing about this job was the hostess I did the trip with, Julia, a Scotswoman with a country girl's face who returned my timid advances. The worst was the boss: a puritanical Welshman, full of beer and prejudices. During the interview he had already given out disturbing signals, babbling on non-stop. The next morning he telephoned me at eight.

'Good morning, Mr Masini, were you up?'
'No.'

'And why not?'

I hung up without even replying: I had to drive his bus at night, now he wanted to test my sleeping morality. He called back at once and offered me the job.

He had it all: servile with the rich and arrogant with his dependants. Thanks to Potter, and thanks to his smug diligence, he could get the bank to lend him money to change his car every so often, to do up the kitchen, to send his children to some exclusive school, and the other amenities which formed the tired repertory of his conversation. Every morning he inflicted on us the jokes they had told on television the evening before and sometimes even lectured us, above all when he felt he had the duty to defend some unpopular choice of the government's. With a paternalism, colonial in its origins, and widespread in the middle classes in the south of England, he had taken on himself the task of teaching even me, a poor Wop without a future, how if you loved your firm and your bosses the doors to riches opened up and you could become like him. In his eyes Italy was an underdeveloped country and he never missed the chance to ask me: 'How often have you changed governments this year?' and then he'd burst out laughing. Or else he'd tell me, half closing his eyes and inspired by passion about the breasts and thighs of a girl from southern Europe (he had trouble telling Spaniards from Greeks and Yugoslavs), repeating threateningly what he would have liked to do to her, biting his lower lip—partly so as not to say everything and partly to have a good suck at it.

THE WAY BACK

Meanwhile Roma was moving on towards the final of some Cup or other: the final was to be played against Liverpool and I hoped they would really wallop them . . . My boss boasted about the English team with such unchallenged presumption that I accepted a bet. For some weeks every single encounter between us was sublimated by raising the stake: by our skirmishes we had reached six hundred pounds, much more than I could afford.

I arrived in the Bar Italia wearing Potter's tartan uniform: I already knew that if they went into extra time I would miss the very end but I had no wish to watch the match among Englishmen. The bar was packed with Italians, like me, out for revenge. To be there, however successful they had been at fitting in, was the result of a defeat. It meant not to have found work at home, to have dreamt too much of some other place, to have problems with the law, their family, their friends, or their city, not to have loved enough the vine-covered hills from which they came, the blue sea and the cement courtyards, not to have been able to hold on to what they had. At least in that bar that is how it seemed to me. We stood there, jammed one against the other as if in Purgatory, and I already knew what we had to say to each other because I had heard before in there and had often said it myself: that you are better off in Italy than in England and the other way round— talk full of interminable comparisons of food, the police, the women, the men. Lots of Armani and Coveri ties, though, so that people can't say we're less Italian than the others. The match begins on a TV set at the other end of the room; I can't see much, but I gather we are attacking when choruses of curses rise up in all our dialects, and that Liverpool are attacking when the room falls silent. *Brothers*, I think, and that I shouldn't feel so emotional.

At half-time some character nods to me, I must have seen him somewhere. He comes over to me and we talk a bit about the match which I have hardly seen. Then he asks me:

'Weren't you a friend of Livio Cavalieri?'

'Once.'

'Did you hear he snuffed it? an overdose.'

The match began again, the players jumped about and at a certain point I had to go. Thirty steps outside the bar and I am once more in a foreign country, the Italian hides in my heart once more while, hurrying through the crowd, my mouth mutters apologies in English if I bump into someone by mistake. I am late, damn extra time, I pass between the wall and a couple who are walking slowly and graze the showcase of a cinema with my forehead. I see Livio, in my mind's eye, sitting on the toilet in my mother's house, and he has fallen asleep with the syringe still inserted in the vein. I jumped on to a bus but five minutes later jump off again, the traffic isn't moving, damn it, I'll be quicker on foot, I must run. I am bleeding a little from my forehead and I have stained the collar of my uniform.

Our boss at Potter's has a very complicated system of fines for the staff: there is one for being late, one for the cleanness of your uniform, another for timekeeping. When I reach the terminal I see him roaming round my bus, flabby and exultant, he is rubbing his hands and singing and spluttering out: 'Liverpool! Liverpool!'

'You'll work for me all your life, Masini—look at this, half an hour late, the collar of your uniform's dirty and you owe me six hundred pounds.' In the garage he begins to chant *Liverpool* again, he must have been drinking. He claps a hand on my shoulder in a more insinuating manner: 'It's the *mamma mia* factor, Masini, the Italians don't know how to win, they missed the penalties. Too much spaghetti,' and he was off laughing again.

I get on to the bus right away otherwise I'll lay hands on him. The passengers are in their seats, the hostess is there too, the one I like, she looks at the cut on my brow and dries it with a handkerchief. 'What did you do?' She is there in front of me but I don't see her, I don't see anything, I am thinking of my boss laughing. I sit down, start up and drive off. I am nervous, I drive very badly, I have entered a roundabout without giving way but fortunately nothing happened. The road is almost empty and will be so till tomorrow morning, till Edinburgh.

Livio, my friend, I still have before my eyes the boys of Roma and Liverpool kicking away and I don't understand. As the miles go past I see coming towards me rapid, broken images of when we were together. We are in the park, we are running on the grass and we fall on top of each other to get our breath back. Your smell. Your voice. 'Are you my friend?' Livio, I am trying to pull you out of a hole, you have given me your hand but I can't manage it . . . They have given you a new motorbike and you come for me outside the house. You call to me from the street: 'Davide.' I look out, I am still eating and I come down with my last bite still in my mouth, the core in my hand. 'Do you want a turn?' You get up behind and from the way you clasp my waist, I realise that you are afraid and I go slowly . . . Then in Trastevere, on one evening like so many others, we are walking along, we are chatting, we are searching. We know all the bars, everything there is to know in the bars: the sandwiches, the pinball machines, the telephones that don't work and give back the token if hit in a certain way, owners who chase you, nice barmaids, who goes where and when. Livio, we have been going about as if roped together, keeping an eye on each other, helping each other to live. We know we are mixing both with snobs and with people who have no future. And in the same way so many others, after hanging about in the bars and squares in their adolescence come down in early manhood from the suburbs to the centre of town. The first Saturday afternoons in via del Corso, as if it were a little provincial town, first records and the first books in the shops in the centre of town, the first evenings after supper. Night, between Piazza Navona and Santa Maria della Pace, it feels as if we were walking through a camp of marauders who have laid siege to the city. Tribes of nomads with their women and of amazons with their men showing each other their hair styles, their cars, their boots, before going back to their bases in Appio, Primavalle, Aurelio or Centocelle. Almost every evening there's a fight, bottles are broken, and in the end the police come. In this world we search like truffle-dogs, we approach people and things inquisitively, we sniff at bodies and souls, with a powerful appetite. From every point in the city a story begins, a trail that is interwoven with others and in the end everything holds together. We'll talk about it tomorrow, Livio, now let's grab it. So we keep on wandering about all night long among the voices, the laughter, the bars, the hours that slip out of our pockets as easily as the few pennies we have, in the streets full of smells and beautiful women, protected by the benevolent rays of the moon until the centre empties and the dawn comes back, deserted by noises, to kill with its first rays anyone who has not found love and is still wandering about. I watch you emerging with the years from the arrogant boy I loved in my own way and become more open, brave, free. In the night sky of our future you trace our dreams aloud and I listen to you. We never spoke so much, it feels as if the world were being reborn in our rambling talk, everything is still fresh in our words and we pick up their meaning with our noses, our fingers, our eyes and ears. A little drunk, but light-hearted, we sing a song as we go back to the bike and every so often a bucket of water rains down but we are merely being born and this holy water envies our gaiety, is our baptism. Livio, Livio, so splendidly unprepared for the life in which I find myself now, in this ridiculous tartan uniform, on this fucking bus! The miles go past under the wheels and measure out the journey, how long it is since we left and how long it is till the end, the moon looks down on our road and the wheel tracks which cut through the heart of the night, the same moon of so many of our roads home along the via Aurelia Antica when the summer wrapped us in the sighs of the park heavy with scents. Livio who had everything, so much richer than me as to make me feel furious and so much more generous that it made me ashamed of my rancour. And from you I learned that we are all the same, we feel the same cold and the same heat, the same hatred and the same love. To you it all seemed easy then: your family offered you on a silver salver interesting careers, journeys halfway round the world, and you came and told me because I too joined in the general enthusiasm for your future and clapped my hands for you. But what is the sense of telling you this tonight when it was you that lost yourself? You, who out of fear of becoming a doctor or a judge *like my father*, would have gone on wandering all your life cursing everyone because they left you, got married, began to work, to think about money. You even called me a slave because I studied, I teased you because you were a rich boy and in that way we lost each other. And yet I knew you were the weaker one, I had always known it, from the time when I saw you begging for everyone's attention, flirting with anyone who flattered you a little, from the day I saw you stammer out your Roman emperors without managing to get two together in the right order and saw your father hug you just the same. I knew that not even a father like that would be able to save you, he hugged you as if to hide his own shame, a fate that he feared for you. You never understood his pity and you stammered ideologies even when they fired at him. Dear friend, I saw you seek death ever since you were a little boy and never understood why. Listen, animals of the woods, nocturnal vagabonds of suffering, brown owls and screech owls, white foxes and blind moles, shadows of the dark which hint at a mystery in the deserted cities. Listen night, our friend, who gathered up our walks and our songs, our dreams told out loud and kept it all in the folds of the sky for other wanderers of the night. Listen to me one more time, silence that receives the secret voices: soon Livio will come to fetch me, we shall drink a coffee at Sant' Eustachio and we'll cross the square looking at the people, the beautiful women and the oddballs. And we'll draw out once more the invisible hours until, the last ones left at the tables along with some stray cat, we'll see the light return from a corner of the sky and whisper to the city to awake.

the threshold of silence

I

We reach Edinburgh: stop, traffic lights, rows of houses closer and closer and higher and higher. It is light already but the street lamps are still lit. The hostess has come up to me, she has laid her hand on the back of my seat and has leant forward a little to guide me across the city. Brushing against her hand with my shoulder I once more entered the climate of expectation of those fleeting moments when by chance we are close. The passengers wake up, take down their suitcases, put on jackets and coats, fasten buttons, knot scarves, they are all on their feet already in the aisle champing to get out. I hear her body like a piece of music and don't ever want to arrive.

While I unload the baggage at the terminal at St Andrews Square I follow her out of the corner of my eye as she hands the trip docket into the office and then as she goes off, alone, towards Waverley Station. The passengers too, having taken their suitcases, quickly scatter. I run in to sign off and immediately come out to look for her. It is the end of May, the air is scented with flowers, the sky is clear, the wind full of vagabond seeds searching for a crack in the earth, the streets white with dandelions. From far off I see her—she has stopped to look at a bed of tulips which are still closed, I needn't run any more, I catch up with her; she steals from the heads of the flowers some drops of dew still intact, shows them to me and says jokingly: 'They were crying last night.' In silence we set off through the narrow wynds that thread their way through the houses of the old city and which every so often look over the valley where the station lies.

'It isn't a valley but the crater of a volcano.'

'There are lots of cities in the Apennines too that go up and down like this.'

'The Apennines?'

Right—why should she know what the Apennines are? and in any case this is not what I wanted to say to her so I mutter 'Italian mountains', making a gesture with my hand as if to get rid of them.

To climb up through a narrow street, I stop to regain my breath. There's a strange smell here.

'It's fermenting hops—there are lots of breweries in Edinburgh.'

As she speaks about Edinburgh she shows pride, takes on a professorial tone. I ask her to tell me some more about the city so as to pursue this unexpected line of erudition. We look at each other often, briefly. But we look at each other, above all through things, pointing them out to each other, following the voices, the breathing, hearing our intentions grow, seeking a way of being. Our eyes would say too much and say it too hurriedly, we must get closer slowly. Every so often however closeness comes to the surface in a glance that plumbs the depth of our expectancy, in a chance contact of our bodies or in an odd word that tries to find a place in the other person: these moments hold us together in an atmosphere of their own, then they run away like the rest of time, go back to the different distances from which we come. Then we talk about other things, like professors, on the surface, as if we were in no hurry to say everything in a single moment. 'Wait a second,' we repeat in our minds, as we secretly approach a welcoming understanding.

She tells me about Rizzio, an Italian musician with whom Mary Stuart had fallen in love and who was murdered by jealous courtiers. 'That poor Italian!' She too must have an odd idea of Italians. She has started to tell me about Edinburgh again but now the trivial pedantry of a tour guide gets in her way, she tries to shake it off with things like 'they say that . . .' and 'it doesn't matter . . .' I feel she is making an effort to be more precise, more sincere. In the tone of her voice there is impatience with the empirical detail of the Sassenachs, she tells with challenging, almost mystical, fervour the legends of Robert the Bruce, Flora Macdonald, Bonnie Prince Charlie. 'We aren't English, do you know that?' I nod but I don't know enough about Scotland to understand what the difference is she is talking about. But I follow her as she tells stories full of myths about these heroes: the protagonists of the legends are like residues of incomplete metamorphoses, ghosts from epochs that burst the seal of the past and thrust themselves out at us. There is something in these stories that defies history, a time that does not resign itself to disappearing and continues to call out, something which has roots in melancholy, in the sense of the end of things. I search for distance, a joke, something to say, but I remain silent and still closer. It would be stupid to make fun of her or to raise objections to her lecture; she is not a scholar, she is setting out her scholastic wares without pretension. Suddenly she breaks off as if lost, perhaps she can't remember how one of these legends is going to end, or is trying to remember something else. Her sentences proceed slowly then she leaves them halfway and falls silent.

'What is it?' I ask her suddenly, I wish she would show me the crevice into which her voice has disappeared. I know I would understand her, it happens to me too that I suddenly can't say certain things. Behind that silence there is something not quite right, something troubles her. She doesn't speak again and without noticing I slip into her thoughts, I feel her confusion, the stories she can't remember properly, the sorrow that even she cannot give the dead a place in spite of memory, the compassion and the legend. Then she breaks out of that silence, I notice the instant when she was about to turn to me to reply 'Nothing' to my question, I know that now she is seeing the valley, she skims over it with a rapid glance and begins to speak to me again, from afar.

'Nothing,' she murmurs. She is shaking off a dream, a state of concentration in which she has been lost: the effort with which she had attempted to communicate these legends to me had thrown her. She had allowed herself to be pulled away beyond this moment into the limbo where ghosts dwell. Slowly, trying to find the thread of her talk again, she begins once more to weave the web that makes me prisoner and reveals her own prison to me. I am aware of every movement of hers as if we were in an embrace. 'Go on talking to me about Edinburgh.'

'I'm not boring you?'

I'm not boring you is coy now: it is her professorial tone and in fact the question falls away at once without a reply like a piece of foam, a residue of the formal attentions one pays to an outsider. The intimacy towards which we are walking, which we are reaching by different roads, has already laid down other rules. If a look or a phrase is false you feel it; you have to go back over the way you have lost. It isn't necessary to speak but what you say cannot be the explanation of something else, it must *be* something else. Now she is telling me about her childhood, she shows me a corner round which there was a certain sweetshop, the house where a friend of hers lived. Through her the city acquires in my eyes hidden details, and through the city I find her again, little by little. She used to run along this pavement with her pockets full of toffees and chocolates, she would look at the people and the houses, she was beginning to know the world; a little of her life has remained bound up with these places, I find her again as she sees them once more in her memory, in a time I shall never know. All these things about *when I was a little girl* indicate a point she wants me to look at and which says: so much is already dead and gone, and I too am merely dying and going away. These are little private ghosts which tell of what has withdrawn into her with time and has become transformed into a nostalgia for herself. I thought she had disappeared into politeness and instead, taking another path, she suddenly appeared before me frank, abandoned to what happens in her heart and is going on around us as if she were already saying to me: 'Don't hurt me with what you know of me.'

To tell stories, to put together again the worlds that have broken into pieces forcing us to continue in a different way, to let another person know us as we know ourselves. I too would like to tell her about Rome, about Livio, about the lost years which now make me so very alone. But for me it is too soon, I wouldn't know where to begin, while for her it is so natural to come towards me.

We come out on to the Royal Mile and while I look at the Tron Clock she leans on my shoulder. I am afraid of not seeing her, of not understanding her, of letting myself be carried away by haste; I call to mind women in tears in my life, their accusations and their reasons, but meantime there is a moment in which this does not happen and we touch each other. I know I am in too much of a hurry, I see Potter's uniform, I know her body is in there and that she is in there too; but my senses overflow, I feel her blood, her organs as before I did her thoughts. I am exaggerating as is my body and this dawn, and the task is to keep everything in this strange calm which is brimming full of complicity. I am searching for the moment when I shall know nothing, will not think any of this at all and we shall be together. I am searching now.

Then she raises her head from my shoulder, takes a couple of steps and invites me to follow her; we arrive at the Castle and from there we go down by steps between walls all black with soot. A chimney puffs out little grey clouds which unravel rapidly in thin arabesques and are lost in the sky and I am happy that everything goes on between these walls, as we walk. Once again I sniff the windborne smell of hops and find myself in a distant dawn: we have been playing cards all night, Livio and I, in Trastevere. Livio has lost a lot of money, with my last hand I came out even, now we are going home. Livio sniffs the smell of bread in the air and stops, like a dog pointing, motionless, searching . . . 'This way, come on, this way.' We go into a little street where the smell suddenly becomes stronger. Another corner and it is very strong, we knock at the window with the light in it, and the baker opens to us in his vest and little hat. He looks at us suspiciously and you ask him whether he'll sell us a loaf of bread, he lets us in, it is February, we warm our hands in front of the oven. We help him to move sacks of flour, we wait for the first batch to come out and talk about Roma, the football team. The baker becomes more affable, in the end he gives us a present of two baguettes and we walk back when it is already morning.

I sniff the wind again, I am seeking the smell of bread but this is beer. Edinburgh is so far away and I don't remember where I can find Livio again. How many commonplace things: how many feelings, how much seeking each other, leaving each other, being there at so many ridiculous moments and not being there when you put a needle in your vein that costs you your life. I hear you calling me in this smell, in the words that come to mind today, after so many years; I know that you too are in that crowd of ghosts who do not resign themselves and which is moving about on the frontiers of forgetfulness, saying, Don't shut it off, not for ever. In a moment she will begin to speak again and you will disappear into the background, beyond memory, like a shadow in the dark. I could follow you, let the events of the day seem like ghosts and make of you, of our friendship and of Rome at twenty my secret cult. But what a miserable consolation that would be when I know that I am deluding myself, that this is the smell of beer and not of bread, that my anger, my regrets and my scruples did not make me do anything to stop your death, for you, because where you were, there is now only an empty space covered by a heap of completely useless memories. This is so simple, clear and insufficient, that reason begins to go begging from everyone, even from those it doesn't believe in: it knocks at the doors of saints and wizards, wonders if along the Milky Way the dead really do reach another world, hopes that someone or something will help the shadow of your life, which was so ill at ease among men, to find a tranquil spot in death at least, in the memories I shall have of you, in the silence in which you are now, where my senses no longer reach you. But I find nothing, reason withdraws humiliated, neither wizards nor saints open the door, it accuses the sense of imagining non-existent odours, the heart of having belated feelings, tells me suffering is a luxury to which I have no right.

She has grasped my hand, I follow her and we arrive at the hotel: she has taken the keys to her room and we go up together in silence. Everyone will be sleeping at this hour. The door closes behind us, she undoes the Potter scarf from her neck, she passes a hand through her hair. For the first time, under a faded perfume, I guess at her body. I keep that smell in my nostrils like the end of a rope and while we undress, a little tired, our gestures being to entwine like so many other threads which could bind us, which we hold on to with the tips of our fingers and we pull on them, coming close together, testing our mouths, stopping, trying over again.

'Pull the curtain,' she says to me, she has sat on the bed and now is taking off her stockings. I go up to her, I look at the nape of her neck through her hair, her breasts, her hands, her skin, her legs. Her body has just revealed itself and it asks for understanding so as to be able to strip itself of shame as well. I undress too and with our first caresses we ask pardon for what we are, if we have a paunch, some wrinkles, if we are afraid or hungry. For having been unhappy and happy, for everything we didn't want to say and for everything we would never know how to say. For the fact that compared to the closeness we now aspire to at this moment, life has already been a betrayal and once more very soon, by falling asleep first or wounding each other by chance, we will betray, we will be alone, with desires murmured or shouted by conscience and not said to you, where I want to be. Forgive me for everything, my friend. I am still thinking and would like not to think. Sometimes a hand grasps me, holds my neck. Caught by gestures all of which say something, all at the same time, and from which we try to learn how to touch and then win trust, she lies down and her legs stretch out, she draws in a breath, on her face savage expressions surface and I see her throw herself down broken paths, abandon the prudent pace at which she had moved through this city and at every breath risk falling, shutting her eyes, stripping off the pieces of the world with which she covered herself. How many ways of behaving have hidden her from me up to now, with what pleasures and pains we confront each other now so that we can allow our guard to drop and give ourselves.

I look at her, I forget, I look at her. Be quiet, thoughts, leave us in peace. Sometimes I admire her, sometimes I glimpse the white of her eyes through the half-shut lashes and I am almost afraid, or else I am only thinking how far she is from me in that pleasure of hers. But I follow the breathing with which she is calling me now, between the open spaces of desire where every gesture is found and dissolves and those tight corners that tie our arms and force us to move. With my ear laid on her back, I listen to the rhythm of her heart and slowly, taking courage, I allow myself to be pulled away from the outside that watches and in which we had begun to touch each other. I see once more her lips drawn back, her expression too, but my eyes are only fragments of something else and of others that fall apart as I slip into her. I feel her advance along the invisible thread of our meeting; she pulls on it again, she holds it as if at some point in her belly a feeling were opening up for her which I cannot touch, a place where opposites part and unite: emotions and lack of passion, concentration and abandon. Everything turns into something else, changes, is transformed, until everything is confused. She pursues and I pursue her, I feel her reach the limits of a state of wholeness in which she finds satisfaction and I hear her breathing slow into longer intakes of breath. Now she lets herself be guided and I seek further, in the dark, for a lost moment and at a certain point I am blind and have lost my guide-dog. The world escapes me, if I move I shall be lost but she knows that already and catches me between her legs, I know that now she is looking and don't want to open my eyes. A silent languor unites us, my dear one, my flesh, you who were a stranger to me and have entered my heart, what will it be like to separate myself from you in a moment? I open my eyes, she begins at every spot in her body, I look at her shoulders, at her eyes under her dishevelled fringe. She smiles, is happy, I stroke her knee, she touches my head and in this way, quickly, we fall asleep in this little bed.

We sleep. Then there is a light, I stare at it for a moment and then realise that now I am awake. The curtain moves slowly, lifted by the irregular sighs of the wind. Noises come up from the street, they are unloading barrels, they are rolling them along. 'Jimmy, aye, Jimmy.' A man has shouted something in a Scottish accent too thick for me, I didn't understand, now they are laughing down there in the street. The smell of fermented hops is still very strong, we must be near the brewery. A bell strikes the half-hour. From the patch of sky revealed when the wind raises the curtain comes the ray of light which, by crossing the flowered carpet, the Potter scarf, and part of my shoe, ends up on the pillow and has wakened me. I have one of her arms round my neck, perhaps because the bed is small or perhaps because she is used to sleeping like that with her husband. I begin to get up very quietly, like a thief, so as not to wake her, but the bed creaks, I upset the bedside table and she opens her eyes wide. I am naked, standing there, I say good day to her and she looks at me in a puzzled way. 'I'm sorry, I didn't want to wake you,' I think to myself in Italian and notice that I am using the formal form of address. Am I already so distant?

'Where are you going?'

'It's sunny.'

'Fine—I'm coming.'

We went for a walk on the Lammermuirs south of the City. There were horses, sheep, cows, a burn edged with wild garlic. She talked to the animals, she knew the names and properties of the plants. I felt on my back the weight of my asphalt streets and of the cement blocks of flats; I had for ever been buried in a city and felt myself alien in front of every plant. Now she was telling me about the unhappy end of the chickens and bullocks, she said pigs were dirty animals only in captivity, how much the ways of these places had changed with the Common Market. I listened to her and when she showed me the swallows I thought how sad it was that one day, at the end of summer, they too would have to go away. 'Did you know they go as far as Africa?' she said and even under the cement of my ignorance of the seasons, the colours and smells, that seemed an extraordinary fact.

She took me to say hello to her somewhat elderly friends: Ian had very beautiful eyes, dark green, veiled by a solemn sadness. The same colour as the grasslands up there, always exposed to the violence of the heavens. He stroked his dog and with his wife made a discreet counterpoint to the story of our walk. Ian talked only about who had sold what and to whom, about what land cost and what it could yield depending on the farming methods, without bothering a great deal about how much we could understand of it. But Margaret kept filling the conversation with gossip: the groom who had made a fortune with an American woman, the wife of the garage attendant who went to confession rather too often, who had emigrated, who had killed himself with too much whisky. They knew my friend was married and tried to find out who I was but, with an elegance that was exquisitely urban, she contrived to divert their curiosity without offending them. They offered us whisky and shortbread, then Ian recited some ballads by Burns about the countryside. To end up my friend sang *The banks o' Doon*.

>Ye banks and braes o' bonnie Doon
>How can ye bloom sae fresh and fair
>How can ye chant, ye little bird,
>And I sad weary fu' o' care?
>Thou'll brack my heart, thou warbling bird,
>That wantons thro' the flowering thorn:
>Thou mindst me o' departed joys
>Departed—never to return.
>
>Aft hae I roved by bonnie Doon
>To see the rose and woodbine twine;
>And ilka bird sang o' its love,
>And fondly sae did I o' mine.
>Wi' lightsome heart I pu'd a rose,
>Fu' sweet upon its thorny tree:
>But my fause lover stole my rose,
>And ah! he left the thorn wi' me.

She sang and her voice swelled rich in colours and air, sometimes rising with agility, unexpectedly powerful, like a bird in a meadow. I still had in my ears the deep breathing of the morning and our embraces: in that song I felt I saw her whole again. 'You should always sing,' I said to her. She looked at me calmly, without escaping.

At the bus station we were still together. The passengers got on, asked for information, she replied politely to everyone, she saw them to their places and as I loaded the baggage I wondered whether we could go on all our life like this, she and I, carrying people up and down along that road. We had no sooner left than she came to sit on a folding seat near me, and told me more about herself and made me happy. Then she curled up on an empty seat and slept for a few hours. For the first time, that night, I felt I was protecting her sleep. The darkness was coming down and certain words came back from afar to settle on my heart like migrant birds getting their breath back on an island in the midst of the ocean. Once again I called on the night animals of the woods, the owls and screech owls, the white foxes, the blind moles, and begged them all not to start up in front of me, not to get killed. She's sleeping, take care.

Dawn arrived when we were on the outskirts of London. She woke up and came back close to me. 'I dreamt we were on the Isle of Skye. I'll take you there sometime.'

I would like to have told her that I had prayed the animals of the woods not to end up under my wheels, that to them I had entrusted my still unspoken hopes, but now that we were drawing near to the city I was only afraid to lose her. Now that other life will begin, she will go back to her husband, more sure of herself. But I wanted her to be with me. I asked her again for the ballad of the evening before and she sang softly so as not to wake the passengers. *Thou'll brack my heart, thou warbling bird*. Rapidly we found ourselves back among traffic lights, the apartment blocks, the police sirens, the flat light of the city, the eternal cement where I come from. My languorous feelings dried up in brusque thoughts and gestures. Throwing down the passengers' suitcase thinking 'your husband', 'the boss', 'the bet', 'damn it'.

I exchanged a few hostile remarks in the garage with a rude passenger, then with the boss, and my heart felt her farther and farther away, doing the jobs that remained and slipping away towards the life into which I could not follow her, to her house, her husband. She couldn't go away like that. But we went out of the garage together as if by chance. We who were united by a sweet necessity now handed over to the violent twists of chance. And yet I could not ask her for anything, not even if she had waited for me, or tell her that I had waited for her or that perhaps we hadn't waited for each other but had still found each other and couldn't lose each other like that.

'Come and live with me.'

'I can't.'

She disappeared down an escalator in the tube in the city where I had lost everything. I set off for my house between two ranks of heroic trees that still managed to breathe on the streets of London, and I missed her.

Enormously. It couldn't end like this, I was sure, but meanwhile, this time when she was far away, her house, the solitude of my next sleep without her, filled me with intolerable nostalgia—all repeated her voice in each fragment, as the unending rails do now that are carrying me away from her. In a gap in the light a bird sang. *Thou'll brack my heart, thou warbling bird.*

Oh Julia!

II

Someone cried out and woke me. A woman's voice, shrill. No, it was the brakes of the train. Here's San Giovanni, we have arrived. Over there is the hospital where my mother died, I still feel the smell of the disinfectants, of the dead, the dying and the half-dead. The doctors, the nurses, the cleaners. Here too, she had won for herself the reputation of an impossible woman. She shouted, I still hear her some mornings when I wake up or walk through the wards of my hospital—an unending echo. The nurses snorted: 'What a bind she is! it's your turn . . .' Once I made a scene. 'Don't you hear the lady calling? suppose it was your mother?' Right—and suppose it wasn't my mother. And how often had I slipped past these shouts so as not to be caught: 'Don't be late . . . don't go too fast.'

In the end I too had got used to the quiet routine of these rooms, to the half-light of the Venetian blinds lowered on a sunny day so that the light didn't hurt someone seeking the shade, to the cautious conversations in which you had to avoid anything that was too much alive, to the silence so as not to disturb people resting; I came every day and like the nurses I knew that she must die, I no longer found this at all strange. You must die, I know you know and that is why you ask me: 'Don't look at me like that.' I tried not to think about it, we go along towards death, there's not much we can say that makes sense. At the end you did nothing but look at the birds outside the window.

It was a strange illness. The doctors were unable to hide a certain academic curiosity: 'How is the lady today?' they asked, hoping that something else sensationally odd had happened to your body. You were unable to resist their curiosity and led them on with your latest biological disasters. Death was so anonymous, slow, perhaps even boring to a lonely old woman like you and you liked to discuss the identity of the mysterious assassin you carried within you. You reported to me too that a case like yours had only been seen in Sweden in 1952 but it wasn't as interesting as yours, the doctor has said so, and you tried to repeat to me some clinical detail. But I was a doctor, I made you feel shy, and so I took away from you the last pleasure left to you—that of talking about your illness. Once when you had got angry because you found I wasn't paying enough attention, you even asked me to kill you with my own hands. 'That way we'll make this damned beast that's gnawing my stomach jump out. At least I'll look it in the face and it's you, my good boy . . .' Me?—what? me your death? People say odd things faced by their own death, but for some days you always went back to being the most loving of mothers, you asked me to tell you what was going on in the world outside there, and I talked until I saw I had lost you again, you had started day-dreaming on your own, watching the birds outside the window, thinking back to some time or other in your life, perhaps about your father, about your flight, about some love affair you must have had but had never talked to me about. I knew so little about you, I had begun to ask you to tell me but you were too tired. To calm me you said that in any case you didn't want to live any longer, the last problem of all was that you just weren't able to give up the days that lay ahead. I was still the only person you had, as I had been all our life together and at this point not even I could do anything about this problem. To give up—that's not life any more. You talked to me about it almost as if to amuse me in some way; I knew that it was only a fantasy, something to talk about, you were so tired of everything that all you wanted to do was sleep, but not even sleep helped you any more: your real death was something else and concerned you alone. Sometimes you were polite in a wonderfully middle-class way: 'Oh thank you, you've come back to visit this old lady! and what lovely flowers you have brought!' I already felt myself enough of a murderer, every day, watching you waste away and unable to do anything for you. I felt I ought to stop you somehow with science and with love, not to allow you to pass over into death. I listened to you cursing your illness, what I or life had been, the nurses, the doctors and I said 'of course', people say odd things when faced by death, we have to understand, and instead I didn't understand that this was your farewell, that this was how you were taking your leave. At the end I spared you even the few comforting things I managed to think up for you because at this moment comfort only made you think of what you would be missing, of how death was the opposite of everything. You wanted to spit on good feelings, on good intentions, to carry down with you into the tomb whatever good things could be said or thought. 'What do you know about it?' You spoke to me as if you were already elsewhere, the pangs of pain returned, you shouted 'Help', and your voice followed me and still follows me along all the corridors, all those shut-off destinies into which I have put my work in an attempt to reopen a way, against madness and death, trying to utter the love which you no longer allowed me to name in your presence.

a stolen suitcase

There is a moment when one wakes up and doesn't know that one exists. When I opened my eyes in the little hotel bedroom, that moment seemed endless to me. It was dawn. That I knew, but I did not remember what place this was and not even who or what it was that found itself there. I had travelled a long time, a customs officer had opened my suitcase and had asked me questions to which I had replied vaguely. His face had come back to me in so many boys in uniform returning from leave. Then the smell of the fields, the pretty girls travelling with their mums, the ones with their fiancés, the ones alone. I had got out at Bologna by mistake and had missed my train: after all that talk to Julia before leaving—I have to go, have to see my country again—I had remained for an hour in a waiting-room looking at people and at the tablet about the massacre without managing to understand why the hell I had set out and to where. I felt as crowded as that waiting-room: the friends and lovers who with time have become people I no longer know, the years of my life in Italy which, without realising it, I carried about with me in a suitcase thus imposing on what I did in England an impossible comparison—years which, when

I really did come back, all disappeared from my mind. Since London I had been getting ready to see Rome again, now I no longer wanted to arrive there and when I finally decided to continue the journey I fell asleep soon after Orte. When the train braked I just had time to see San Giovanni. No upsetting emotions, no nostalgia. Perhaps Rome is always as crude as this: while I was looking for Sandra's number in the phone book in a booth in the station they nicked my suitcase. It was a question of a second; I was keeping an eye on it because I know what the Stazione Termini is like, I looked at everyone suspiciously. I left it behind me for a moment while I was looking in the phone-book, I probably took fifteen seconds, and I felt that it was gone. I turned round suddenly, I looked at the people in the station, I took a couple of steps towards the crowd but realised at once that it was useless: they all seemed to have a suitcase like mine and yet not really mine. It had disappeared, there was nothing to be done. Fortunately I had my passport, my identity card and my money in my pocket.

I had not much stuff in that suitcase—a pair of shirts, underwear, a book I wanted to give as a present and an old suit. I walked down through Monti and bought the bare necessities; toothbrush and toothpaste, shaving cream and razor, a shirt and another pair of underpants. Then I took a room. That is where I had found myself on waking, but it is difficult to give a good picture of the moments of awakening because to think and narrate takes up a certain time, while that feeling of absence was timeless. Now time would set off on its forward march again and I with it. But the journey here had blurred this linearity; people had come to mind, whom I believed had disappeared from my life, as if nothing had ever gone away and, on the contrary, had merely accumulated, throwing into relief certain episodes which had been the landscape of another journey across the years which had taken me far from Italy. I was not clear why I had come back to Rome, but I knew why I had left it, or at least that is what some thoughts said which I had found in my pocket like a couple of keys I had looked for in vain all over the house. But these thoughts were dreams and now for good or ill I was waking up, leaving them behind.

I got out of bed and was happy to wash and put on the shirt I had bought the evening before, to fasten to my wrist this time which is all made up of hours and minutes and to find distraction from the confusion of my waking by looking out at the hotel window which gave on to the street. Now Rome pleased me, there was only a dustman in the street and I could see the topmost stones of the Coliseum. I went out at once to find a bar to have breakfast, I had arrived, I didn't want to go anywhere else, now I had to try to put to good use the little time I had at my disposal.

On summer mornings like this Sandra and I often said goodbye in the street after making love all night in a hotel bedroom like the one where I had wakened. I want to call her. But can one turn up years later and say I know I didn't send flowers for your birthday and not even a letter, but I thought about you? say: I remember the scar you have behind your ear, I would like to see you.

They are full of loves like ours, the cities: loves for which you have to hide, have to watch what you say and to whom, can't give yourself away and do nothing but give yourself away. They are loves without a history, about which nothing can be said, which leave only moments, scraps left over from the important things you always think ought to be done. Loves to be lost in hotel bedrooms, in glances exchanged in a bus or in the street, which repeat to the secret of solitude that you have been happy and could be so again even if you don't believe it at all, only to recall that there is a moment which evades the rules and the weeping and wailing and is always there, round the corner of the street, keeping a question open. I would 'phone but later. Now it was the streets that summoned me more than anything else and spoke to me of Rome. I looked out on the Forum from behind the Mamertine: my memories have all become old, they found it hard to give themselves a face. But these thousand-year-old street corners wore their age like children, how many revolutions, how many successes and failures, how many loves and murders had pursued each other down these streets. With what tenacity men and women had tried to come to terms with the world so as to be able to say of them, as of these columns, I am something that does not pass away.

Instead everything human had passed at a great rate among these stones, facts had dissolved into personal opinions, accounts by secretaries, courtiers, memories, lies. No one—not even Nicola—knew any longer who he was; which was all the better because now he had changed his name and opened a pizzeria in Paris. The beautiful women whose myths we had sung were now mature mothers, people who had rushed around arrogantly on Vespas, braving the wind and the streets, now had a comfortable car and worked in an office. We had all grown up, in ways that were the same and different, and this did not displease me. The fresh morning air bathed my face. I had a thought that whistled away in my mind and said more or less: I too have already passed on and what I have before me is something else, other people, the new world that is born every morning. A world in which we certainly continue to wash and wash ourselves, to clean, to arrange things and rearrange them, to ask 'How are you?' and to say 'Fine' or 'Not well'. A world of teeth, hands, bellies full and empty, thirst sleep hunger, smoking and stopping smoking, never having smoked, never having given it a thought, of always thinking thinking and thinking even when you think you aren't thinking. A world of other tomorrows, other yesterdays, today, days before and days after, which crumble in our pockets as we run along. A world in which out of sleep we arrive different every morning, ready and not yet ready, inevitably present.

I would ring to see Sandra again, and even if I didn't

know with what coldness or warmth she would receive my call, I at last saw that my journey had meaning. One passes so much time muttering about what one has in one's suitcase, about who one is, what a person has and what one has done in life, what one wanted and what one would like, but is happy only when that suitcase is stolen. Only when one no longer feels in another person's glance the weight of who one is, or feels in the walls of a city which is dear to one the ghosts fade away, and sees what has happened finally be left behind. And today I am that person.

There was a bar open at Torre Argentina full of students and office workers. I listened with great pleasure to their Roman cadence. I come from here, I thought, I still have that accent when I speak Italian. Soon I would leave again for London where I worked and where Julia was, yet nothing would have deprived me of the dearly loved traits of my people, from which I came and among whom, after so much wandering, I was arriving. Nothing could take away from me the nostalgia for a love, the world which had passed through me and had not ended in the void, had formed me, had given me all I had. Even if a past world does not return I knew that it lived in things like a secret and was their richness, what filled them with meaning. I paid for my cappuccino, got a phone token and called Sandra who made a date for that evening at Turiddu's.

the bill

'Hey Turiddu, what about that bill?'
'Coming!'

The table is covered with breadcrumbs, the chairs have been moved a little back from the table to form little after-dinner groups and allow our bodies a gentle reminiscence of the Latin nostalgia for the triclinium. While we wait for the bill the conversations continue but are more tired, they drag on in weighty repetitions, codas in search of a resolution. Someone is asking a favour of someone and has already taken his wallet to treat him to the meal, 'May I?' The other resists briefly, next to him is someone else who is yawning, rubbing his eyes, looking at his watch and then at a woman. Can it be his wife? Soon he will ask her again 'Are you ready?' thus implicitly begging her not to be led off on further wanderings to someone's house or some club. Or else she is a woman he would like to woo but up to now his efforts have got nowhere from indolence, too much food, scant imagination and bad temper and have ended in a consolatory monologue and so he is letting her know, by a yawning ellipse, that he has given up. At another table a voice is firmly putting an end to a discussion with 'Next time you are in Rome call me and we'll settle things,' providing a counterpoint to the hesitations of his interlocutor with various expressions of 'No, seriously', which are indispensable because his tone of voice instead affirms his desire to get away from the bore. At our table Sandra lost her head when Fabio Cavalieri arrived but the others are calmly reaching the end of the evening.

Finally Turiddu appears and calls together the drowsy ones and the dreamers, the petulant ones, the phlegmatic ones and the chatterers. He has his notebook in his hand and is going back over the dinner methodically: the cover charge, the wine and bread, the hors d'oeuvres, the entrées and so on.

'But who had the consommé? is somebody not well here?'

'Hey, Turi, what bill is this you're doing? didn't you go to university?'

'What do you mean? At the Sorbonne, but the French don't know how to eat, forget about them. I used to make our best stuff for them—fettuccine, some tomato sauce, abbacchio, instead these savages wanted me to stick béchamel on everything and different kinds of mustard. Let's get on and what's this—a saint honoré? Forgive me, sir, but you're not French are you?'

'Oh Turiddu, you've got it in one this time, he's from Dijon.'

'I'm so sorry, sir, I didn't mean to be rude, but what can I do if you only eat puddings? And then I'm like that, these people know me, I always say what I have to say.'

'Forget about it, Turiddu, do this bill.'

Other protests arrive, someone remembers to say that the endive was special and Turiddu was off talking about his cousin at Ceri. It is he who is breaking up the company and he knows it, the bill paid the groups will dissolve and he too by now has almost finished his work. He would like to tell more stories, jokes, become his clients' friend. He knows however that someone is trying to take advantage of things, and then he brings matters brutally to an end. Another manages to say to the person who was trying to reduce the price while Turiddu was clearing away the coffee cups: 'Must you always make us look like beggars?' and suddenly Turiddu, re-emerging from the tough way he had slapped the bill on the table, mutters: 'I'm offering the liqueur.'

It isn't expensive. It's still an old-fashioned business with grandmothers and aunts in the kitchen and various sons and nephews serving. And Turiddu, naturally, who is by now an institution in Rome.

We pay, we get up. I help Sandra to put on her jacket and for a moment keep my hand on her shoulder, stealing from her a little intimacy, a little of what we were. I think of Julia. Tomorrow I shall leave. Then we go towards the cars, Fabio and Giacomo ahead, Sandra and a certain Walter who, I think, is with her behind me. It is a warm night in early summer. In the air there is a strong scent of pines and oleanders which brings to mind nostalgia for something, and the desire to tell someone of it.

Founded in 1986, Serpent's Tail publishes the innovative and the challenging.

If you would like to receive a catalogue of our current publications please write to:

FREEPOST
Serpent's Tail
4 Blackstock Mews
LONDON N4 2BR

(No stamp necessary if your letter is posted in the United Kingdom.)

Also published by Serpent's Tail

Appearances
Gianni Celati

Appearances is a book of four novellas that play with the distinction between appearance and reality. Like Borges and Calvino, Celati never loses sight of the fact that a good story is one that entertains and, whether describing the ups and downs of the rugby-mad Barratto, the conditions of light on the Via Emilia, the disappearance of a respectable man or the students in Milan bent on discovering the true meaning of books, the four novellas in *Appearances* are a dazzling blend of storytelling and philosophical speculation.

'*Appearances* provides further evidence of Celati's originality. These novellas are more introspective than the stories, tinged with philosophy and, at times, extremely comic.' *TLS*

Also published by Serpent's Tail

Voices from the Plains
Gianni Celati

'An extraordinarily beautiful book . . . [Celati's] unusual talent is among the most impressive in contemporary Italian letters.'

PAUL BAILEY in *The Observer*

'Celati's richly varied narratives are thoroughly modern in content and form . . . his translator has skilfully conveyed the simplicity of his laconic style, combining fullness of detail and extreme concision.'

TLS

'His generous, panoramic vision imparts a fable-like quality . . . This English-language debut merits serious attention — and applause.'

Publishers Weekly

'His quietly understated glimpses of these sobered, stunted lives has a moving cumulative power.'

Philadelphia Inquirer

Also published by Serpent's Tail

The Voice of the Moon
Ermanno Cavazzoni

It could be that his name is Savini: what is certain is that wells talk to him, colonies are obsessed by echoes and deserts are saddened by melancholy. This is the situation in normal times. At full moon, things really get out of hand. He falls for a lady with a hungry beak, Napoleon is routed in an orchard and Garibaldi loses his memory. A delightful story, *The Voice of the Moon* reflects the appearances that lie behind reality. Its wry humour is truly Fellini-esque.

Also published by Serpent's Tail

The Gangsters
Hervé Guibert

The narrator, Hervé, returns to Paris tormented by a painful attack of shingles, to discover that Louise and Suzanne, his two elderly great-aunts, are being terrorised and robbed by a gang of extortioners posing as building workers renovating their house. He calls in the police, but the investigation fizzles out in a morass of inertia, buck-passing and covert racism.

Wearied, ill and sliding by degrees into paranoia, the narrator leaves for a holiday. With him goes Vincent, a friend whose ambiguous and menacing presence has become increasingly oppressive and who, at the end of the book, may — or may not — murder him.